John Culpepper, Esquire

Lori Crane

John Culpepper, Esquire

Lori Crane

Copyright 2015 Lori Crane Entertainment
All rights reserved, including the right to reproduce this book or any portion thereof in any form whatsoever.
For information, please email LoriCraneAuthor@gmail.com.

Published by Lori Crane Entertainment
Cover design: Robert Hess
Editor: Elyse Dinh-McCrillis at The Edit Ninja

www.LoriCrane.com

This book is a work of historical fiction.
Some names, characters, places, and incidents are from historical accounts.
Some names, characters, places, and incidents are products of the author's imagination.

ISBN: 978-0-9903120-9-3
eBook ISBN: 978-0-9964295-0-4

John Culpepper, Esquire

Family Lineage/Cast of Characters

John Culpepper 1606-
John's wife: Mary Culpepper
　Children:
　　Henry Culpepper 1633-1675
　　　Henry's wife: Elizabeth Green
　　　Children: Robert 1664-
　　　　Henry Jr. 1669-
　　Dennis "Denny" Culpepper 1637-1664
　　James Culpepper 1639-
　　Robert "Robbie" Culpepper 1641-1664
　　John "Johnny" Culpepper Jr. 1644-

John's brother:
Thomas Culpepper 1602-1652
　Thomas's wife: Katherine 1602-1658
　　Children: Anna Culpepper 1630-
　　Alexander "Alex" Culpepper 1632-
　　John "JJ" Culpepper 1633-
　　Frances Culpepper 1634-

John's cousin:
Lord John "JC" Culpepper, 1st Baron of Thoresway 1599-1660
JC's son: Lord Thomas Culpepper, 2nd Baron of Thoresway 1635-
Lord Thomas's wife: Lady Margaretta van Hesse 1635-

King Charles II 1630-
Queen Mother Henrietta Maria 1609-1669
Sir Edmund Plowden 1590-1659
Sir William Berkeley 1605-
Sir Samuel Stephens 1629-1669

Table of Contents

1650, Accomac, Virginia Colony	9
1650, The Dockyard	13
1650, Visitors	25
1651, Chesapeake Bay	33
1652, Edmund Plowden and Thomas Culpepper	39
1652, Commissioners	51
1652, The New Patriarch	57
1653, Katherine and Alex Return to England	67
1654, London	73
1656, France	79
1658, Katherine St. Leger Culpepper	84
1658, Death of Oliver Cromwell	89
1659, Lancaster County, Virginia	91
1659, London	97
1659, Margaretta van Hesse	101
1660, Margaretta and Alex	107
Spring 1660, Governor Berkeley	111
May 29, 1660, The King Takes the Throne	115
January 30, 1661, Posthumous Execution	123
1661, Susannah Willis	125
1663, The Culpepper	133
1664, Storms	147
1667, Albemarle, Carolina	159
1668, Anna Culpepper Danby	167
1669, Samuel Stephens	171
1669, Henry Culpepper, Jr.	177
1670, Frances and Will Berkeley	181
1670, Catherine Culpepper	185
1672, Fishing	193
Author's Notes	199
Books by Lori Crane	205

About the Author 207
Excerpt from *Culpepper's Rebellion*, the fourth book in the
  Culpepper Saga 209

CHAPTER 1

1650, Accomac, Virginia Colony

"Sir Edmund," the servant called across the busy tavern.

Edmund Plowden was sitting alone at a table in the back of the Tan House. He looked up and saw his stable hand standing in the doorway. "Over here, boy. What is it?"

The boy approached the table. "Sir Edmund, you told me to tell you when John Culpepper returned to Accomac. His ship docked early this morning, sir."

"Very well. Thank you for letting me know." Plowden took a drink of ale.

"He's got a ship full of people with him, sir."

"What kind of people? Settlers?"

"No, sir. I heard him refer to one of the men as brother and another as son."

Plowden slammed his mug down. "That's

just what this colony needs—more bloody Culpeppers." He spit tobacco on the floor and wiped his mouth on the sleeve of his shirt.

The outburst caused the room to quiet. Plowden and Culpepper had been enemies for nearly two decades. No one talked much about it as no one liked Plowden, but everyone knew. Plowden had been jailed in England for the physical abuse of his pregnant wife, but he escaped while on his way to court and ended up in Virginia. He fled England to avoid prosecution and paying alimony, but since he had been in the colony, he'd spent more time in court than out of it. He had been involved in more than forty court cases in Virginia, but none was bad enough to land him in jail. He was simply an offensive man with a violent temper and sour disposition. Most people called him a bully, but never to his face. The only reason everyone knew about his past in England was because John Culpepper was the lawyer who had represented Mabel Plowden, Edmund's wife, and Culpepper had made no secret of what an unfortunate example of a man Plowden was.

John Culpepper, on the other hand, was a pillar of the community. He ran a merchant vessel between England and Virginia, delivering much needed wares to residents of the colony and contributing to their income by selling their tobacco and cotton in England. He also assisted his friends and neighbors with their legal matters. He was a gracious man in his mid-forties, a distinguished member of the gentry who had always held British propriety and manners in high esteem. Other men admired him, and the women thought he was one of the most attractive gentlemen to ever grace the shores of the Chesapeake. His prowess as a sailor had not gone unnoticed by the female persuasion. His tanned face, graced by dark curls and piercing blue eyes, was the subject of many daydreams.

Those who overheard the conversation between Plowden and his servant were glad Culpepper was back and anxious for any news about the state of England. King Charles had been tried on charges of treason and the high commissioners found him guilty as charged. In an act unprecedented in the history of England, the king was beheaded on the Tower Green on January 30, 1649. The colony had received word that the king was dead and Oliver Cromwell was now running the country, declaring the land the English Commonwealth, but the settlers had heard nothing more. They didn't know where the king's heir was. They didn't know if their families in the homeland were safe. They didn't know much of anything, as it took months for word to travel between the continents.

A few gentlemen in the inn hastily rose and left to go speak with Culpepper. Others waited for word to filter to them through other means. With a wave of his hand, Plowden rudely dismissed his servant and ordered himself another ale.

CHAPTER 2

1650, The Dockyard

John led his wife down the tilted gangway, walking in front of her as she held on to the back of his woolen coat. He could usually navigate the complete gangway in four or five steps, but she was moving so slowly, he had to take dozens of tiny steps to allow her to keep pace.

"Be careful, my dear. The gangway is fairly steep, and I'm sure you don't have very sturdy land legs right now."

"How long will it be until my head stops rocking?" Mary asked.

"It'll be a few days. After being at sea for six weeks, it may take some time for you to get your balance back and stop spinning."

"Do you experience this woozy feeling every time you sail?"

"A bit, but I've sailed so many times, I just ignore it until it goes away."

"Father!" Henry called from the upper deck. "Should we begin unloading the ship?"

There wasn't much to unload as John's ship had sailed to England to rescue the family and didn't stop at any ports to secure new merchandise, but he couldn't expect Henry to know that. "No, Henry. The crew will take care of it. Come down here and help your mother."

Seventeen-year-old Henry, the eldest of John and Mary's five sons, ran across the deck toward the gangway. John thought Henry's long hair, trailing behind him, should be tied back and out of his face, or better yet, cut, but he admired Henry's maturing physique, his muscular arms, his face bronzed from being on the ocean. The boy had developed into quite a good-looking young man while John sailed back and forth across the Atlantic, staying in Virginia for months on end and leaving the rearing of the boys to their mother. In John's long absences, Mary had raised their boys in John's brother's home. Thomas was undoubtedly a respectable substitute father and a remarkable role model for the boys, but John didn't know how he would ever repay Thomas for raising his children and watching over his wife. Now that they were all together in Virginia, perhaps he could find a way. John had grown up without his father in his life and had vowed to never allow that to happen to his own children, but somehow the years passed, and the boys had grown in John's absence. John had spent years feeling guilty about not being at home with his sons, but there wasn't much he could do to resolve the issue. He was a merchant and merchants didn't make money sitting at home. His boys meant everything to him, and he knew he had fallen immensely short on his vow to raise them.

John had sailed his merchant ship to England to rescue his brother Thomas, who was a colonel in the king's army. Following the disastrous civil war and the king's subsequent beheading, Thomas was now considered a traitor and one of the most wanted men in England. Parliament, under the direction of Oliver Cromwell, had seized the property of all royalists, including the vast lands and stately manors that belonged to the Culpeppers. Cromwell also controlled the docks and the waterways, abruptly bringing John's merchant business to a screeching halt. Since Thomas was named a traitor, the whole family was in danger. Cromwell's men would certainly retain any of them to find Thomas and place his head on the executioner's block. Since John snuck into the country to save his brother, he was more than likely considered a conspirator, a treasonous offense, and would undoubtedly warrant a place next to his brother on the scaffold. None of the Culpeppers would be able to return to England for a very long time, if ever. The Culpepper family would need to remain in Virginia, and John would now have to make a living as a lawyer, using the skills he so fervently hated learning while growing up. He wouldn't be able to resume his trades with England for quite some time, probably years, possible decades.

John heard his youngest squeal on the deck and figured one of the older boys was picking on him. John glanced up but couldn't see the child over the high bulwark. Johnny was six years old, a rambunctious boy who had known no peaceful childhood. Johnny had been born in the middle of the war and seen and heard things children should be protected from. He had grown up hearing details of battles and fighting, traitors and executions. John got the distinct impression during their voyage to Virginia that his son was growing into a bit of a rebel. On their long ocean journey, Johnny had picked fights with the other children, acting out the stories he had heard. John wished he could go back in time to give the boy a nonviolent infancy. Maybe it wasn't too late. Now that the family was all together, Johnny would grow up with his father in his life, a benefit the rest of John's boys never had. Perhaps John could get his youngest to stop being such a strong-willed little imp.

John and Mary finally reached the end of the creaking gangway and carefully stepped onto the wooden dock. They both turned to watch Thomas guiding his wife and two teenaged daughters from the ship onto the gangway. Thomas led the way with one daughter tiptoeing after him, followed by his wife, and finally his second daughter trailing at the end of the line. The girl's faces were pale and their expressions looked worried. The three women held hands, their knuckles white and their arms trembling. In their colorful dresses, bonnets, and curls, they looked like fancy island birds sitting side by side on a fence railing.

John thought he had never before and would never again see such a funny sight. His sister-in-law, Katherine, smiled at him as she inched her way toward the dock. She was surefooted and obviously happy to be nearing dry land. If she hadn't been assisting her frightened daughters, John imagined she would have strolled surefooted down the walkway as if she had climbed on and off ships a thousand times.

John's nieces were another story. Sixteen-year-old Frances and twenty-year-old Anna held on to their mother's arms for dear life, gripping her so tightly they nearly stopped her from moving forward. Thomas softly reassured the girls that they would momentarily be on dry land, but they had both been so green with sea sickness for the entire voyage, John knew it would be a while before they felt normal again. John wondered about the girl's behavior on the ship and suspected they weren't as sick as they claimed, but were merely whining for attention. Admittedly, the journey was long, the girls were bored, and the accommodations were harsh.

They had spent six weeks living without the finery they were accustomed to, but their incessant grumbling was more than a little frustrating for everyone within earshot of them, crew and family alike. John wasn't used to being around spoiled girls and cherished the fact that women weren't welcomed on ships for just such a reason. Fortunately, the girls were not his problem, so he ignored their moans and complaints and left them to their mother.

"Thomas, do you need a hand?" John called.

"No, we're fine." Thomas rolled his eyes.

When the shuffling women finally reached the dock, Thomas sat the girls down on two wooden crates and told them to stay there until he returned for them. Surprisingly, they didn't complain about getting their dresses dirty on the dusty boxes. They sat quietly and watched the rest of the family disembark.

Henry bounced down the gangway next, holding hands with Johnny. Johnny, an excited grin on his face, looked around the dock, ready to pull away from Henry's grasp at any moment to run and explore. Henry held him tightly. When the two reached solid ground, Henry led his little brother over to Frances and Anna. "Would you like to sit here with the girls, Johnny?" he asked.

Johnny nodded and Anna held out her arms for him. He crawled onto her lap.

Henry turned to John. "Father, where do

we have to go from here? I am anxious to see your home and your warehouse."

John pointed north where a dusty road, not much more than a path, led into the spindly pines. "It's not *my* home anymore, son, it's *our* home now, and it lies about two miles up this road. I've already sent one of the sailors to go get the wagon to carry the ladies. He'll be back shortly."

"Good. I'm excited to see your property."

"*Our* property, Henry," John corrected as he looked up at the ship. "Benjamin!" he called to his first mate on the deck.

"Yes, Cap'n," Benjamin yelled over the side.

"Where are my other sons?"

"They're up here learning to fold the sails."

"Well, send them down as soon as they're finished. We need to get the ladies to shelter before nightfall."

"Aye, sir."

Within the hour, the sailor had returned with the wagon pulled by a dappled gray mare. The wagon was nothing more than a few decrepit wheels held together by rotting boards. It was decorated with bits of hay, tobacco, wood shavings, and dirt, but at least the ladies wouldn't have to walk. John loaded his wife, sister-in-law, and two nieces into the back. He apologized to them for the crude transportation, but fancy carriages were something they would not find in the small fishing village of Accomac, Virginia. The journey to the family's house would be bumpy and dusty, and the wagon would surely be cramped and uncomfortable, just like the ship had been. Sadly, there was absolutely nothing John could do to make them more comfortable. In the past, John spent only enough time in Virginia to provision his ship for return. He never needed more than a place to lay his head and was quite content with his meager accommodations. Today, for the very first time in his life, he dreaded the arrival at his two-room shack. To say it was modest was being extremely generous. It was a hovel, and it'd be an eye-opener for John's aristocratic family, especially the spoiled girls.

The residents of Virginia worked hard to survive, particularly out here on the peninsula. They did not live in great splendor. They barely lived in comfort, and most lived in absolute squalor. There were no manor houses, no servants. There were no silks and laces. John knew the ladies would not find his small dwelling suitable, but he hoped he wouldn't have to remind them that relocating to Virginia was a necessity to save Thomas's life. If they all worked hard enough, their situation would soon improve. Lord knows it couldn't get much worse.

Once the ladies were settled in the rickety wagon, John picked up little Johnny and hoisted him up on his shoulders. He then grabbed the reins of the mare and pulled her forward, clicking his tongue as he did so. The wagon's wheels grinded softly. "This way, gentlemen," he said to his brother and the boys.

Thomas hurried forward to walk by John's side. "It's quite beautiful here, John. Reminds me of our grandfather's property."

John chuckled. "That's exactly what I thought the first time I saw this land. My house is nothing like the grandeur of our grandfather's, but something about this place feels like home."

"Well, it is home for all of us now."

They walked in silence for a while as John wondered where he would house his brother, four women, and seven boys. At least his family was safe from the turbulence in England. They wouldn't be rounded up and charged with treason. They wouldn't be hung or beheaded here in Virginia. And truth be told, they had nothing left in England. John and his family would start over...somehow.

The boys walked behind the wagon, commenting on each shack and store, each tree and flower with excitement in their voices. An old gray donkey that John had become well acquainted with over the years brayed as they passed, and the boys stopped to pet it. It wagged its string of a tail and tried to nip at the boy's shirtsleeves, making them roar with laughter.

"John..." Thomas began as they paused.

John pulled his attention away from the boys and turned to his brother.

"I just wanted to say thank you. Thank you for getting our families out of England, and thank you for saving my life."

"You don't need to thank me, Thomas. You've taken care of my family for years. It's the least I can do to try to pay you back. And you're the one who helped me buy that ship sixteen years ago. I guess everything happens for a reason. Turns out that reason was to save your hide." John laughed, trying to lighten the tone of the conversation.

"He was furious with me, you know."

"Who?"

"Father."

"For helping me buy the ship? You never told me that."

"I don't think he was as mad about the actual ship as he was that you had sailed away, and he was terrified you'd never return."

John stared straight into the trees before them. "I guess in his world, I never did return."

"I felt awful that he died while you were away."

"I didn't." John pulled the horse and walked forward.

Thomas watched his brother walk away. John's tone had abruptly ended the conversation.

After another half mile, little Johnny, riding atop his father's shoulders, patted the top of John's head and pointed to the right. "What's that?" he asked.

John lifted the boy off his shoulders and set him on the ground. He stopped the wagon in front of a tiny shack built of logs. "That, my boy, is your new home." He turned to the ladies in the wagon. "Ladies, may I present Casa de Culpepper."

The ladies in the back of the wagon stared at the shack, unmoving. Anna's jaw dropped open.

"This is your house, Uncle John?" Frances asked.

"I'm afraid so. I only built it large enough for myself, and I wasn't expecting company." He walked around the back of the wagon and helped Mary down. "But we'll fix it up."

"Fix what up? It's a shack," Frances said.

Her mother shushed her. "Frances, your manners."

John ignored the girl and smiled at his wife.

Mary didn't smile back.

John Culpepper, Esquire

CHAPTER 3

1650, Visitors

The following morning, the sunlight filtered through the threadbare curtain covering the single window in the main room of John's home. John pulled the edge of the curtain back and peeked out the window. The foggy mist from the previous night had burned off, and the songbirds were out in full force. It would be a beautiful day.

He tiptoed past his nieces, who were sleeping on the floor, and found his wife had lit the wood-burning stove and was warming cider in the kitchen area.

"Good morning, my dear," he whispered and then kissed her cheek.

"Good morning, husband. So, this is how you live when you're not at home?"

He shrugged and looked around. He had offered Thomas and Katherine his own bedroom and sent the boys to sleep in the loft of the warehouse. His nieces snored softly in front of the fireplace, where the roaring fire had dwindled down to white ashes overnight. Mary had slept on the lumpy sofa and John had slept in his chair with his legs propped up on a small coffee table. Besides a dining table with three mismatched chairs, that was the only furniture in the room.

John leaned back to ease the stiffness from his lower back, realizing that sleeping in that chair was not going to be a solution for long. He took in the room with new eyes, realizing his wife must be appalled by her surroundings. The dining table in the corner of the kitchen area was covered with supplies—ropes, wood scraps, bits of tattered sails. The single kitchen counter was filled with various tools and pots and cups. The washbasin was filled with dirty dishes that had been collecting dust and flies since John sailed to England to save his family over three month ago. Mary took the pan off the stove and poured the cider into two cups. "I know it's not the grandeur of Greenway Court that you're used to, but until now, I haven't had any need for more than this."

"I'll try to organize things today. Maybe we can make this place livable."

John watched her place the pan back on the stove, then pulled her into his arms, and looked into her brown eyes. "I know this isn't grand, but at least we're all alive and all together. We'll make it work. I'll set the boys to building more rooms, and I own five hundred acres north of here where we can build Thomas and Katherine their own home."

She smiled up at him, causing the lines around her eyes to deepen. "I don't care about grand. I don't need a manor house or a castle. I only want to be with you. I've watched you sail away for sixteen years, and each time I wondered when or if you would ever return." A look of sadness crossed her face. "I don't want to do that anymore. I don't want to ever do that again. I want to stay by your side." She glanced around the room. "Even if it's in this...this fleapit."

"It's not that bad."

Mary smiled. "Yes, it is."

"Well, my dear, it's *our* fleapit."

He kissed her lips and felt her relax in his arms. He tangled his hands into her hair and hugged her tight to his chest and sighed. He was happy they were together and relieved their long ordeal was over. The bloody war was finished, and the subsequent escape from England was behind them now. They could finally live in peace. John's serene thought was interrupted by a gunshot outside. They both jumped and looked toward the front door.

"What the—stay here," he commanded. He let go of her and grabbed his rifle from the mantle. Frances and Anna stirred.

"What's going on?" Frances asked, sitting up and rubbing the sleep from her eyes.

"Stay there," John said to the girls.

Thomas emerged from the bedroom and stood in the doorway buttoning his trousers. "Was that a gunshot?"

"I think so," John answered as he opened the front door.

Morning sunlight blazed into the small room, a rectangle of warmth washing across the floor and the girls. Thomas grabbed his pistol off the dining table and tucked it into the waist of his pants. He followed his brother out the front door and pulled it closed behind him.

"So, the rumors are true," Plowden roared from atop his horse. "It's a bloody Culpepper invasion." He swayed a little as if he had already been drinking this early in the day. He was flanked by his two scraggly-haired henchmen who sat astride their horses, grinning. The brothers seldom left Plowden's side, and the appearance of the trio usually meant trouble.

"What do you want, Edmund?" John bellowed.

"I came to see if what I heard was true. You've brought your family over from England."

"What's it to you?" John asked, his jaw twitching as he clenched his teeth.

"Oh, I just heard you were carting a pretty maiden. You know I'm always looking for a future Mrs. Plowden. Thought maybe I'd marry me a Culpepper wench." Plowden smiled and next to him, one of his cronies cackled like an old witch with breathing problems.

In one fluid movement, Thomas whipped out his pistol, aimed it at Plowden's head, and cocked the hammer. The click silenced everyone.

Plowden didn't react, but his associates simultaneously drew their pistols and pointed them at Thomas.

After a few tense moments, Plowden smirked and asked, "Now what shall we do?"

Thomas didn't flinch. His pistol remained pointed directly at Plowden's head. "I don't know who you are, sir, but I would advise you to stay away from my daughters."

"Daughters? Plural? You mean I have my choice?" Plowden threw his head back and roared with laughter.

John reached over and slowly pushed down on the short barrel of Thomas's pistol. "Don't let him rile you up, Thomas. He's nothing but a troublemaker."

"A dead troublemaker," Thomas corrected. He glared at Plowden, but he reluctantly allowed his brother to lower the weapon. He took a step toward Plowden's horse. "I am Thomas Culpepper, a lieutenant colonel in the king's army, and I will eagerly blow your damned head off if you even think about touching one of my daughters."

All of the men turned to the sound of an approaching horse. A large brown stallion galloped into the middle of the yard, carrying Sir William Berkeley.

"Oh, it looks like you have company," grumbled Plowden. "I'll take my leave, Culpepper, but I'm sure I'll see you all again very soon." He winked at Thomas. "Tell your girls I look forward to meeting them." Plowden yanked on his horse's reins, kicked the beast in the ribs, and galloped in the same direction Berkeley had come from, sneering at Berkeley as he passed. The brothers followed him, hooting and hollering as they disappeared into the pines.

Berkeley pulled back the reins and halted his horse as he turned to watch the troublemakers ride away. He then turned back to John. "I'll ask you later what Plowden and his buddies were doing on your property, but first I came to see if it was true. You've brought Thomas back with you!" He dismounted from his horse and walked toward them.

"Yes, it's true." John turned to his brother. "Thomas, you remember Will Berkeley from Middle Temple, don't you?"

Thomas tucked his pistol into his waistband and walked forward, his hand outstretched. "Oh, of course, I certainly do. It's been twenty-five years since our school days. It's nice to see you again, Will."

Berkeley shook Thomas's hand and patted him on the shoulder. "Has it really been that long?"

"I'm afraid so." Thomas smiled.

"It is so very good to see you again, Thomas. I heard things went quite poorly in

England."

"Well, if beheading the king fits in that description, then yes, it went quite poorly."

"You'll have to fill me in on all that's happened over there. I've heard rumors that Cromwell is sending someone here to take my place. He doesn't want any supporters of the Crown in charge of the colonies."

"In charge?" Thomas asked.

Berkeley waved his arms around. "I am the governor of this magnificent land."

"Oh, now that you mention it, I seem to remember John telling me that. You'll have to forgive me, Will, it's been a long war in England and an even longer escape to come here," Thomas said.

Berkeley turned to John. "Yes, you'll have to tell me all about that adventure, too."

Mary stuck her head out the front door. "Husband, is everything all right?"

"Yes, dear, everything is fine. Come out and meet my oldest and dearest friend, Sir William Berkeley."

Mary stepped into the yard and Berkeley approached her, reaching for her hand.

"Mary, this is my friend Will. Will, my wife, Mary."

Berkeley gently took her hand, kissed it, and held it to his chest. "My dear, you are as lovely as John always said. Now I know why he was always in such a hurry to sail back to England."

Mary blushed.

"Welcome to Virginia," Berkeley continued.

"Thank you," she said.

Berkeley looked past Mary to the door. Frances and Anna stood in the doorway, their hair disheveled from sleep. "And are these your daughters, John?" he asked.

"No, I have all sons. These are Thomas's daughters."

Berkeley turned to Thomas. "You're going to have to keep your eye on these lovely girls, Thomas. I think I now understand why that scoundrel, Plowden, was here."

John shook his head. "Plowden's not getting anywhere near them, and they're too young for you, too, Will." John laughed. "Let's go inside and have some hot cider, shall we?"

CHAPTER 4

1651, Chesapeake Bay

It took nearly a year for the family to expand John's shack into a respectable house they could live in comfortably, although by the time they finished it, the boys had made themselves comfortable in Virginia and were seldom home. Henry found great pleasure in making friends and roaming the countryside for days at a time, and little Johnny was always running off, forcing his mother to look for him. She usually found him down the road, terrorizing the old donkey.

Thomas and Katherine built a house on John's land north of Accomac and moved their children up there. Their new home wasn't nearly as grand as the nineteen-room Greenway Court where the family lived in England, but they settled in nicely.

After a year of working on houses, barns, and gardens, John and his family were finally beginning to feel a sense of normalcy. On one rare occasion that the family was all home, Mary cooked a delicious chicken dinner and called John and the boys to come to the table and eat. John said a blessing over the meal and was carving the bird when Henry said, "Father, Mother, I have something I'd like to tell you."

"Can it wait until I've finished carving, Henry?" John asked.

"I'm sorry, Father. I'm just so excited to tell you my news."

Mary rose from her chair and took the carving knife from John's hand. She smiled at him and indicated with a shift of her head that he should pay attention to his son.

John sat back down in his chair and raised his eyebrows toward Henry. "It's obvious you're about to jump out of your skin. What is so exciting?"

Henry grinned. "I've decided to move west and explore the country."

Mary dropped the carving knife. When she fumbled to retrieve it, she knocked over her husband's glass of water. The liquid ran off the table and into John's lap. He jumped up from his chair.

"Oh, I'm sorry," Mary said as she grabbed her napkin and tried to dry the mess that was darkening his trousers.

John grabbed her hand, "Stop. It's fine."

She pulled away from him and began wiping off the table. John sighed and sat back down. No one said a word as they watched her feverishly sopping up the water. The tension was so thick, no one around the table moved. The boys looked down at their plates and began eating. John watched his wife. When Mary finished cleaning up the spill, she retrieved the water pitcher from the counter and refilled her husband's glass. After she returned the pitcher to the counter, she marched into her bedroom, slammed the door, and didn't come out for the rest of the evening.

The next morning over breakfast, Mary told John in no uncertain terms that he needed to stop Henry from moving away.

"No, Mary, I'm not going to behave like my father and decree to my son what he will do with his life. The boy is eighteen years old. He's a man. Let him do what he wants."

"I wish you would for once in your life act like his father and tell him this is unacceptable. This is the first time the family has been together for any length of time, and I don't want him to go."

John looked down into his cup, deeply hurt by her words. When he looked back at Mary, he said, "I don't know what you mean by *act* like his father. If you mean you want me to dictate his life like my father tried to dictate mine, I'm not going to do that, and that's the end of this discussion."

Mary softened her tone and tears filled her eyes. "I'm sorry, John. I didn't mean for it to sound like that. It's just that this is the first time in eighteen years we've been together as a family, and I don't want to see my firstborn running off to live on his own. I'm his mother and I don't want to lose him."

"Mary, we've been together for a year, and it's been a good year, but maybe it's time to let Henry go live his life. He wants to become his own man." John rested his fork on the edge of his plate, placed his elbows on the table, and folded his hands under his chin. He cocked his head at her.

She looked into his eyes. "I'm being selfish, aren't I?"

John nodded.

She sipped her cider, gazing over the rim of her cup at her husband.

"You should be glad." John resumed eating.

"Glad about what?"

"This came about because Berkeley told Henry the French have a lucrative fur trade with the Indians in the West and that he should go explore that area, but after you pitched such a fit last night over the idea, I had a long talk with him and advised him to check out somewhere a little closer to home. There's beautiful land in Lancaster County and it's only across the bay from us, only a short sail on the small boat. Not more than a few hours. He can return home anytime, and we can visit him anytime you'd like. He has agreed to look into it, and you, my dear, need to let him grow up."

She tore a bit of bread from the loaf. "The other side of the bay would be a little better, I suppose." She sighed. "I'm going to miss him, that's all."

Henry entered the house at that moment and wiped his boots on the rug. "Miss who?"

John grinned at Mary and then looked at his son. "We were discussing your move."

"Oh, Father, I'm so excited to tell you the latest news." Henry poured himself a cup of cider and sat down at the table. "This morning, I spoke with Bill Greene, my friend from town, and he said his father owns land in Lancaster County and will allow us to build on it. We talked of opening a livery to make money and planting tobacco. Bill also has experience as a blacksmith, so we may do that, too."

"You don't want to buy a ship and become a merchant like your father?" John teased.

Mary gasped.

Henry laughed. "No, sorry, Father. I like it better on dry land."

"Well, maybe one of my other sons will follow in my footsteps. Denny and Robbie both seem to have a fondness for the sea."

"I feel for their future wives," Mary said under her breath.

"Why? Sailing is a noble profession." John sat up straighter and feigned insult.

"Of course it is, dear. I'm just teasing

you." Mary turned to her eldest. "So, Henry, when are you thinking of going to Lancaster County?"

"Probably early next week."

Mary put her hand up to her chest, her breath coming out in jagged gusts.

John looked at his wife's beautiful but worried face and shook his head ever so slightly. He looked at Henry. "Son, you let us know if you need anything."

"I will, Father."

CHAPTER 5

1652, Edmund Plowden and Thomas Culpepper

Thomas and Katherine spent their first year in Virginia building a beautiful home on the five hundred acres John owned. They began their second year building a barn to house animals and to dry tobacco. Frances and Anna, now eighteen and twenty-two, respectively, helped Katherine decorate the modest home with beautiful tapestries and quilts, and their sons JJ and Alex, who were nineteen and twenty, helped plow and plant the tobacco field.

The home wasn't nearly as splendid as their former home in Kent, but they were comfortable. Frances frequently protested about the amount of chores she was required to do, but her father reminded her repeatedly that remaining in England with their servants would have resulted in his beheading. She always apologized and remained silent for a few weeks, but as time passed, the complaining would slowly begin again when her spoiled ways got the better of her.

Except for Frances's grumbles, the family comfortably eased into the community, becoming active in the local church and frequently visiting the local market to buy or sell produce. Thomas, an experienced lawyer, even joined the court that met once a month at the Tan House in Nassawadox. The establishment, so named because of its color, was twenty miles south of Accomac and was the place where all matters of business were held.

Throughout the last two years at the Tan House, Thomas had spent more time hearing cases against Sir Edmund Plowden than any other man. Each time he read Plowden's name on the docket, his stomach churned. John was right—someone should run that mischief maker and his two cohorts out of town. It seemed Plowden was nothing more than an intimidator, bullying residents relentlessly. Thomas remembered John telling him about Plowden when John had represented Plowden's wife against her husband back in England. Thomas had thought at the time that no one could possibly be that contemptible. He had since learned he was wrong.

The two misfits who followed Plowden around were brothers who looked as if they hadn't seen a comb for at least a decade. Their appearance was appalling with their stringy, knotted hair trailing down their backs, their unshaven faces, and the folds of their necks caked with dirt from not bathing for more time than anyone would ever care to estimate. In lieu of spending time on self-care, it seemed Plowden and his associates spent their time searching for opportunities to break the law, their offenses ranging from drunken brawls to threatening shop owners to stealing their neighbor's livestock, though there was never any proof of the latter.

Plowden's personal activities were even worse than those of his cohorts. He had spent a lot of time in court charged with not paying workers he had hired and had even been accused of forgery when he tried to convince everyone he was the owner and governor of New Albion. The ownership documents were forged, but no one could prove Plowden was the one who forged them, so he was never punished. Plowden always paid his fines and never did anything bad enough to cause being incarcerated or placed on public humiliation in the stocks, but the members of the court, especially Thomas, were tiring of him and his gang's mischief taking up their valuable time. Plowden's latest escapade was destroying a local tavern in a fit of drunken rage.

At the end of Plowden's hearing, Thomas rose from his seat and addressed the assembly, demanding the court do something about the time Plowden was taking from other town business. Other members of the gathering rallied in agreement and the magistrate nodded.

The magistrate asked Plowden to rise, and Plowden did so. The magistrate bellowed, "Sir Edmund Plowden, you are to pay for the chairs you smashed and you are to replace the broken front window of the tavern, along with five shillings and fifty pounds of tobacco which you will pay to the owner of the tavern for his inability to make an income until the property is restored. An additional five-shilling fine will be paid to this court for taking up our time yet again. As Mr. Culpepper has stated, we tire of seeing you in our courtroom. If you appear before this court again, it's quite possible you will be looking at time in the bilboes, followed by a public whipping until you express remorse for your behavior. We will not tolerate any more of your unruly conduct in Accomac." He slapped his gavel on the desk. "Court is dismissed."

Plowden rose and glared at Thomas, mouthing the words, "You'll pay." He then turned and stomped toward the door, his boots clunking loudly on the wooden floor. He allowed the door of the Tan House to slam loudly on his exit.

"I don't like the way he looked at you," Berkeley said to Thomas under his breath.

"Oh, he can look at me any way he wants. He'll be in shackles soon enough. We see him in court nearly every month and the magistrate warned him."

"Plowden is a despicable character, and since he's recruited those brothers to do his dirty work for him, the three of them together are certainly trouble for anyone who crosses them. They are incapable of staying out of trouble, and I'm sure we'll see him back here next month."

Thomas nodded. He wasn't the least bit intimidated by Plowden and his cronies. He had seen far worst behaviors during the war in England. He had seen his royalist friends executed before his very eyes. He had seen good men blown right off their horses by cannons. He had even seen the king beheaded and watched his royal blood ooze down the front of the executioner's block. God rest his soul. There's nothing Plowden could do to make Thomas nervous. Plowden was nothing but a hot bag of wind and would surely pay for his unruly behavior soon enough.

The members of the council rose, shaking hands and bidding each other a good day. They left the building two by two. Thomas and Berkeley found themselves alone in the room and they chatted for a while about local business and were the last to leave. When they reached the front door and stepped out into the sunshine, gunfire rang out. Berkeley looked up and down the road, across the street toward the general store, next door toward the church. It was then he saw a man with long hair on the other side of the bushes in the churchyard, aiming a pistol directly toward him. He ducked down as a second shot was fired. The shooter jumped on his horse and galloped away. Berkeley didn't get a good look at the man's face, but he thought it was one of Plowden's henchmen. Berkeley turned and found Thomas lying at his feet, blood soaking through the front of his white shirt.

"Thomas! Someone get the doctor," Berkeley screamed.

* * *

"John, why would someone do something like this?" Katherine cried as she sat at her husband's bedside.

"I don't know. If it was Plowden's doing, I wouldn't be surprised. He doesn't need a reason to hurt someone." John's teeth clenched in anger as he stood over his pale brother. "I promise you, Katherine, if it was Plowden, he won't get away with this."

Berkeley had told John that Thomas had lost so much blood by the time they got him to the doctor, he looked as white as one of John's sails. The doctor said the bullet had gone straight into Thomas's lung and removing it would probably kill him. He tried to stop the bleeding as best he could and told Berkeley there was a very slim chance Thomas would survive.

He allowed Berkeley to take Thomas home to his wife and to die in his own bed. Katherine hadn't left her husband's side since the moment they arrived in the wagon.

John pulled back the blanket and looked at the blood-soaked bandage wrapped around his brother's chest. Most of the blood was on the left side of Thomas's chest. The doctor said if the bullet had struck him an inch to the right, it would have pierced his heart and killed him instantly. John grimaced. Maybe that would have been better. John gently replaced the blanket, feeling his own chest constrict from seeing his brother in such a state.

"Katherine, send the boys to get me if you need anything. I'll come back in a few hours. Maybe Thomas will be awake by then." He gave his sister-in-law a brief but tense hug and left.

John rode to his house, walked into his living room, and sat down on his couch. The emotion he was trying so hard to hide for Katherine's sake erupted from his chest. He bawled like a baby. Mary entered the back door and found her husband bawling. Heart-wrenching moans escaped his throat. She sat down on the floor in front of him and wrapped her arms around his knee.

"What am I going to do?" John sobbed.

"What do you mean?" Mary asked softly.

"My father ran my life for the first twenty-five years, and Thomas has run it for the last twenty. I've been happily sailing on my ship, not a care in the world, because I knew Thomas was taking care of everything—including you and the boys. I haven't had to take care of anyone but myself—ever." He looked into Mary's eyes. "Thomas is going to die, Mary. I don't know how to be a man in his place. I don't know how to be the patriarch of the family. Katherine is going to look to me for answers and I have none to give her."

"Don't worry about that now, John. We'll get through this together. No one expects anything of you."

"They will." He wiped his cheek with the back of his hand. "They'll want to know how to survive. How to build. How to plant. How to harvest. I've been sailing since I was twenty-seven-years old. I don't know any of those things. What happens when Thomas's girls need to be married off? How do I find them husbands? I've never done any of this before."

Mary rubbed his knee. "Husband, there is plenty of time to figure all that out. Right now, the only thing you need to do is stay strong for Katherine. The rest will work itself out." After a moment, she asked, "Why did you come home?"

"I came to see if you would go back with me to help with Katherine." He sighed. "I don't even know how to comfort her." His shoulders slumped as he looked down at the floor.

"Of course I will. Let me grab the soup I made for them and we'll go right away. How is Thomas doing?"

John shook his head.

A tear rolled down Mary's cheek as she rose from the floor.

* * *

John returned to his brother's house with Mary in tow and found a tearful Katherine sitting on the steps of the front porch, her eyes red and puffy. She hadn't left Thomas's side since he was brought home, so John dreaded the fact she was sitting outside alone. They climbed down from the wagon and approached the porch.

"He never woke up," Katherine said calmly. "He's gone."

Mary sat on the step next to her. "Oh, Katherine, I'm so sorry." Katherine started sobbing and Mary held her.

John froze in the middle of the yard, feeling his heart crumble in his chest. He didn't know what to say. He didn't know what to do. Only four years his senior, Thomas had been more like a father to him than a brother. How would he survive without his brother? How could this happen?

Finally, John climbed the steps and rested his hand on Katherine's shoulder for a moment before entering the house. He stepped inside and turned back to look out across the field. *Who will harvest all that tobacco?*

He stopped for a moment in the parlor

where Thomas's children sat together. They looked at him with tear-stained faces, but no one said a word. No one knew what to say. He left the room and went down the hall to Thomas and Katherine's bedroom. He slowly, hesitantly, opened the door and approached Thomas's bedside. A tear made its way down his cheek as he reached down and touched his brother's hand. It was cold. John cried.

For hours he sat at the side of the bed, staring at his brother, his friend. There was nothing he could do to make this right. It was a nightmare from which he couldn't awaken. Hours later when Mary came for him, he followed her through the empty parlor and onto the front porch. Above the tobacco field, he noticed the sky lightening. The sun was rising just over the horizon. It was almost dawn. A new day. A day without Thomas.

While the family prepared Thomas's body for the funeral, John rowed his small boat across the mouth of the bay to Jamestown. He went straight to Berkeley's office to inform him of Thomas's death. When John entered the room, Berkeley looked up at him from his seat behind the desk.

"John, I can tell by looking at you."

John nodded. "It's over. He died last night."

"Have you slept?"

John shook his head. "I came to see that charges are filed against Plowden."

"I'm a step ahead of you, my friend. I had a posse looking for him and his men all day yesterday, but they weren't located. We'll continue looking today...and tomorrow, if need be."

John exhaled at the bad news. What if Plowden got away? Who would make him pay for this tragedy?

"John, I was the only witness and I can't say for certain that it was Plowden's men who did this, but we'll find them and question them. I didn't see those boys in town yesterday, but I promise you, we won't stop searching until we get the truth."

John nodded.

John Culpepper, Esquire

CHAPTER 6

1652, Commissioners

The day of the funeral was gray and drizzling. John stood at the head of his brother's coffin, staring down at the wooden box sitting in the mud. The water dripped from his soaked hair onto his cheeks and mingled with his tears. He didn't bother to wipe the drops away. He could feel the presence of Katherine and her children on one side of him, his wife and sons on the other, but he couldn't bring himself to look at any of them. No matter how much Thomas's wife and children loved him, they would never be able to understand what he was to John. He felt so alone now.

The men slowly lowered the coffin into the ground and the people in attendance walked by to pay their final respects. The entire village of Accomac and a large part of the population of Jamestown had come to pay their respects. John absentmindedly shook hands with them as they passed.

After the burial, he heard the minister deliver words of condolence to Katherine and her children, for all the good those would do. John finally gathered the courage to look up at his sister-in-law and his nieces and nephews. He had never had anyone rely on him before, and the thought hit him like a tree falling—he now had two families to care for. Thomas had watched over Mary and the boys for years. John knew returning the favor was the least he owed his brother, but he didn't even know where to start.

Anna cried silent tears, her handkerchief covering her mouth, her shoulders shuddering. Frances was more dramatic, sobbing loudly and accepting hugs from anyone who would offer one. Should John go to them and hold them? He'd never raised girls. He wasn't sure. What would his father do? Why did *that* thought even cross his mind? He knew exactly what his father would do—disappear for the rest of the day and not comfort anyone. The thought angered him. He tried to push it aside. He didn't want to spend this day thinking about the father he so despised. What would his grandfather do? He'd been a loving man, a kind man. He would be strong and patient with the family. He would support Katherine and her children to the best of his abilities, both financially and emotionally. He would make sure they were well taken care of, not only for the moment, but for their futures as well. He would find good husbands for Anna and Frances to make sure they had men to look after them and to assure they lived the rest of their lives in the style they were accustomed to. Yes, that's what his grandfather would do. Was it more important to see to the family or to find Plowden? John didn't know the answer to that question.

Later that evening, John sat in his kitchen with Berkeley. Berkeley had told him there was no word on Plowden's whereabouts. The suspected murderers seemed to have disappeared.

"If Plowden fled England to avoid paying his wife alimony, I can only imagine how fast he would flee Virginia to avoid murder charges. Good riddance to him," Berkeley said.

"You're right, Will. I don't think we'll find him anywhere in Virginia, but I vow to one day find the man and exact revenge for my brother's death. Even if Plowden didn't pull the trigger, I'm convinced he's the one behind it and he'll pay for this."

"Don't do anything rash, John. I don't have a lawyer good enough to get you out of charges for killing Plowden. Let us handle this."

John knew Berkeley was right. John couldn't afford to get into any trouble and be taken away from his family. He was the patriarch now. He nodded to Berkeley, indicating he understood, and realizing he was so devastated by the loss of his brother, he probably wasn't thinking clearly.

Thomas had been in the prime of his life. He would have been fifty years old this summer. He left behind a beautiful wife who loved him very much. He left behind Anna and Frances, who were old enough to marry but loved their father too much to leave home. He left behind his sons Alex and JJ, who were old enough to exact their own revenge. The thought suddenly occurred to John that he would need to speak with the boys and make sure they also kept level heads.

"There is other disturbing news," Berkeley said after they finished talking about Plowden.

"What?"

"As I knew was coming, Oliver Cromwell has sent over two commissioners to take my position as governor. The parliamentarians who killed our king are now coming over to rule our colony."

"Oh," John groaned. "Why doesn't he just keep his business in England? He's already messed up that country to his liking."

"I know, but he has sent Richard Bennett and William Clairborne to act as the commissioners now, so it looks like I'm retiring as your governor."

John looked toward the dying embers in the fireplace and shook his head. Could life get any worse? He looked back. "What about finding Plowden?"

Berkeley shrugged. "I'll do what I can as long as I am in office, only another few weeks."

"What are you going to do with yourself now? You're not going back to England, are you?"

"No, I don't think I'll ever go back. I guess I'll retire to my estate at Green Springs and live the life of a leisurely, country gentleman."

"Can I ask you to do one thing before you retire?"

"Sure, John, anything."

"I'm going to find husbands for my nieces since they no longer have a father to protect them. I want them to be securely married with good husbands."

Berkeley grinned. "Are you asking me to marry one of them?"

"No, no, I already told you you're too old for them. I'm asking you to make sure their marriage certificates are filed before you go."

"Of course I will. Bring them to the courthouse in Jamestown and I'll see to it before I leave for Green Springs."

"You're a good friend, Will. You always have been."

"Not good enough to find and punish Thomas's killer."

"Don't worry. We'll find Plowden and his men. They'll have to come up for air sooner or later." John rose to add more wood to the fire.

Berkeley nodded. "Like I said, keep your

head and don't do anything illegal. I don't want to see you in the hangman's noose."

"I'll do what I have to do."

CHAPTER 7

1652, The New Patriarch

"I don't want to stay in Virginia, John. I want to return home," Katherine said as they sat in the rocking chairs on the front porch of her home, watching the sky in the east darken as the sun behind them began its descent.

"I don't think that's a good idea. We don't even know what state the country is in right now."

"I don't care about Cromwell or your politics. I want to go home." She rocked angrily in her chair, causing it to knock loudly against the wood porch beneath. She stared out across the road at the tobacco field. John could tell she was trying not to break down and cry again.

"Katherine, first of all, this is home now. England will never be home again. Everything is gone—the houses, the lands. Things aren't going to get better just because you return, and he isn't going to come back because you step foot on

English soil."

He watched her jaw twitch as she clenched her teeth. Perhaps he was being too harsh, but he needed to continue.

"Second of all, I'm concerned for Anna and Frances. There are no longer any eligible men in England. The gentry has been all but wiped out by Cromwell. I think the girls should marry here. They will have brighter futures in Virginia."

Katherine stopped rocking, her knuckles turning white as she gripped the arms of her chair. She turned and looked at John. "I don't care if you are the new patriarch of the family, John. I want to return to England and I won't leave my daughters behind."

"But their future in England is less than questionable, Katherine. If you go, you will return to squalor, and I can't in good conscience allow your daughters to live like that. They shouldn't have to suffer any more than they already have. Any suitable family with young men their ages would have been decimated by the war, just like our family, unless of course they served Parliament, in which case those people are our rivals. Thomas would turn over in his grave if one of the girls married a parliamentarian. And the Culpepper name is certainly not welcomed in England any longer. We are now enemies of the state."

"I told you, I don't care about your politics, John. I want to return home and I want my daughters to come with me." Tears filled her eyes. John couldn't tell if they were tears of sadness or anger.

"You're grieving and not thinking clearly. The girls will become old maids there."

"We'll live in a hovel in London if we have to. I don't want to stay here."

John sighed, not knowing how far he should push Katherine while she was grieving so deeply, but he knew he was right. There was no future there for Anna and Frances.

Katherine's voice rose. "I don't appreciate you shoving your newly acquired family power down my throat."

John spoke calmly. "Katherine, I'm not shoving anything, but I've lived in both places for two decades. I know how this works."

She didn't respond and the silence between them was unbearable, but John remained quiet and gave her room to sort through her feelings.

Finally she spoke, "I guess I don't have a choice, do I?"

"Please don't be angry with me. I'll arrange passage for you to return if you wish, but the girls have no reason to go to England." He leaned forward and looked down at his boots. "I never wanted this power. I never wanted to be the family patriarch. I certainly never wanted Thomas to die."

"Of course not," she said softly. After a moment, she squared her shoulders and sat up straight. "You don't have any more choice in being the family patriarch than I now have as to where my daughters will live or who they will marry." She rose and went into the house, slamming the front door.

* * *

A few days later, John returned to Katherine's house, hoping she was a little more clear-headed. They sat alone at her dining table. She didn't offer him anything to eat or drink.

"I'm not going to force the girls to marry without your consent, Katherine, but I'd like you to meet two gentlemen who can offer the girls bright futures."

He told her about Christopher Danby and Samuel Stephens, explaining how they would be good matches for Anna and Frances. After he reassured her that he wouldn't coerce the girls into marriage against their will, Katherine reluctantly agreed to meet with the gentlemen.

"You are not the only one with news, John. Alex has agreed to escort me back to England and to find us suitable accommodations, even if we have to live in London proper. I wish to leave Virginia as soon as possible, with or without my daughters."

John was stunned. "I'll help you as much as I can, but you know Thomas lost everything. He forfeited his money, manors, and lands in the king's service. He died a hero—a destitute hero.

That's one of the reasons the girls should be married here. If they want any sort of good life at all, they should agree to the unions. You need to give them your approval and encourage them to marry—for their own good."

"I realize that and I know Thomas didn't leave us anything. As a matter of fact, I'm embarrassed to have to ask you for passage for myself and Alex."

"Of course, I will give you whatever you need, but please understand, my funds are not unlimited. I haven't run my merchant business in two years. I lost everything with the end of the war also."

"I understand," Katherine said. She looked down at the floor. John didn't know if her expression was one of sadness or frustration or a little bit of both.

"Katherine, please stay until the girls are married and then I will purchase passage for you and Alex to return to England."

She looked up at John and nodded. Through the pain in her eyes, he saw her slowly accepting the fact that she couldn't support her children—here or in England. She would have to let the girls go, and she would probably blame John for a very long time.

"Did you talk with JJ?" John asked.

"Yes." She sniffed and looked down at the woodgrain of the table. "He wants to stay here. He's hoping you can help him find a job so he won't be a burden to you."

"I can do that."

John was saddened by Katherine's pained expression. A few weeks ago, her family was sitting down to supper at this very table. Now they had been destroyed, decimated by a senseless act of cruelty. He hoped someday Katherine would forgive him for insisting the girls stay in Virginia. He was certain once she met the young men, she would feel better about the arrangements. Both men were gentlemen of exceptional breeding, highly regarded in the community, and had bright futures. They could give Anna and Frances prosperous lives.

Christopher Danby, whom John had chosen for Anna, was the son of Sir Thomas Danby. They were English landowners and politicians. The Danbys, like the Culpeppers, had chosen the king's side during the civil war and had lost nearly everything, but Christopher's mother's family had not taken sides. They still owned ten manors and over two thousand acres of land in England. Perhaps someday Christopher and Anna could return to England and bring back the splendor of the aristocracy. After meeting the soft-spoken young man, Katherine approved of the union, and Anna was quite taken with the handsome young man. It was obvious by their smiles that the attraction was mutual.

Samuel Stephens, chosen for Frances, was a native-born Virginian. He was the son of Richard Stephens and Elizabeth Piersey

Stephens. John knew Richard Stephens from the Virginia council. He was an upstanding gentleman and a member of the House of Burgesses. His son, Sam, was a landowner in his own right, holding vast acreage in Albemarle, Carolina, owning all of Roanoke Island, and managing a sixteen-hundred-fifty-acre estate in Elizabeth City, Virginia called Boldrup. John had taken Katherine to the estate to meet Sam, and Katherine was pleasantly surprised by its grandeur. Upon marriage, her daughter would live in the style in which she was raised. She would have an enormous manor house complete with servants. Also, there were rumors that Sam Stephens was next in line to become the governor of Albemarle. With Cromwell's recent rulings and his pawns changing places on a whim, one couldn't be certain, but imagining her baby girl as the possible first lady of Albemarle, Katherine gave her blessing.

* * *

Two weeks later, the family gathered at the courthouse in Jamestown, where the girls were wed to the young men, and Governor William Berkeley signed and filed their marriage certificates. Tears were shed, paperwork was in order, and it was done.

After speaking with John about Katherine's immediate plans to return to England and the need of her youngest son to find employment, Berkeley appointed Thomas's youngest son, JJ, as assistant surveyor general of Virginia. The lad was young for the appointment, and the position was not much more than a formality, but it was the best Berkeley could do for the family, and final act as governor.

Following the marriage ceremonies, Anna remained in Jamestown with her new husband. Katherine promised to write as soon as she found a place to live in England, and Anna promised to come visit her as soon as her new husband said it would be safe to do so.

Outspoken and dramatic Frances boarded an ornate carriage with her new husband and moved away to his plantation in Elizabeth City. Boldrup was a vast and prosperous plantation and Frances was now a very rich woman. If she behaved herself and kept her spoiled complaints in check, she could someday be a very important woman in the future of colonial politics. She certainly had the personality for it.

The next day, JJ packed his belongings and went to live with the surveyor general to learn the tools of the trade. He was excited about the opportunity, assuring his mother he would be just fine. He told her the current surveyor general was quite aged, so eventually JJ would probably rise to the position himself. Katherine was tearful, but she was pleased for her children.

Upon returning to Accomac, Katherine packed her meager belongings into a small trunk. She had arrived on the shores of Virginia two years earlier with her husband and four children. She and Alex would be leaving with broken hearts and not much more.

John Culpepper, Esquire

CHAPTER 8

1653, Katherine and Alex Return to England

The Jamestown dock was bustling with sailors and ships and John felt his heart race at the sights and smells. "Alex, you're a brave young man and I'm proud of your for taking care of your mother." John hugged the young man.

"Thank you, Uncle John. I think the first thing I should do is check on Leeds Castle and see if it's still in our possession. Mother would love to live there."

John shook his head. "I wouldn't count on that, Alex. My uncle Alexander left the castle to you during the war when you were a minor, but only if your father was alive to oversee it. If the family still owns it, it belongs to my cousin, JC, now."

"But isn't JC in Denmark or France or

somewhere with the prince?"

"Last I heard, he was in Russia trying to raise an army and get the prince on the throne. I'm not positive where he is now, but whether Cromwell seized the castle or it still remains in the possession of the Culpeppers, it's not yours any longer. You'll have to find another place for your mother to live."

"I'll find her a comfortable place, Uncle."

"I know you will." John patted him on the shoulder and they turned to walk toward Mary and Katherine who were saying their goodbyes in front of the massive ship.

The four hugged and John watched the ladies give each other a final embrace and wipe away each other's tears. Katherine walked up the gangway, turning around to look at Mary when she reached the top. Alex followed and wrapped his arm around his mother's shoulder. Once they were aboard, two burly sailors pulled the gangway away from the ship and the boards crashed against the ground with a roar. The sound made everyone jump. Katherine placed her handkerchief to her lips and sobbed.

Seagulls cawed overhead and the warm breezes caressed John and Mary's faces as they stood on the dock and watched the sailors cast off the lines. As the sailors began to raise the sails, he heard Mary sniffle next to him and he wrapped his arm around her waist. They tearfully waved good-bye to Katherine and Alex until the ship disappeared around the bend of the James River.

"What are we going to do without them?" Mary asked.

"I'm sure they'll be fine. I'm sure things in England have calmed over the last few years. Perhaps Alex will soon send word that I can return to London and resume my merchant business."

"Don't you have enough business dealings here with all the legal issues in the colony?"

He took her hand and they turned to walk toward their waiting wagon. "I've certainly been busy but of course I'd love to get back to the sea. Watching Alex sail away on that ship pulled at my heart."

Mary didn't respond.

John glanced at her. Perhaps he shouldn't have said anything about the sea. He imagined that the thought of him sailing away after the loss of Thomas and now Katherine's departure was too much for Mary. When they reached the wagon, he took her elbow to assist her. After she was seated, he squeezed her hand and looked into her eyes. "It'll all be fine, my dear."

She nodded.

He walked around the wagon and climbed up.

Once they were comfortable, Mary said, "I hope they'll be safe once they arrive. Alexander Culpepper is probably not a name Parliament will be happy to hear."

"I imagine by now Parliament has rounded up all the royalists they intend to. At least I hope so. It's been three years. I'm certain they'll be fine. Alex will take good care of his mother."

"I hope so." Mary watched the wharf dwindle from a bustling center to nothing more than a bordering storage area filled with barrels and crates. The sounds of dockworkers and sailors faded into the distance behind them. "I thought for a moment they could live at Leeds Castle. I miss Uncle Alexander," she said. "I haven't thought of him for such a long time. He was a good man."

"He certainly was, and a brave man, too. We've lost many, my dear." Thomas's bright smile flashed before John's face. His eyes filled with tears and he turned away from Mary to hide his grief. After he composed himself, he reached over and patted her knee. "We'll go on as we always have."

Once they reached the entrance of the James River, they boarded their small boat and sailed across the mouth of the bay to the peninsula. Then they climbed aboard their rickety wagon for the final leg of their journey home. The wagon bounced up and down on the dusty road while the sunlight filtered through the trees. The old donkey brayed as they passed. John glanced at it with no expression. It usually made him smile, but his heart was so heavy, he wondered if he would ever smile again. They rode silently, with only the sound of grinding wheels and the occasional huff from the old mare accompanying them.

"Why are you so quiet, dear?" John asked as they neared their house.

"I was wondering if I'll ever see Katherine again."

"Perhaps you can sail with me when I go back to London—*if* I go back to London. Let's wait and see what Alex has to say once they get there."

John knew Mary had no intention of ever sailing the ocean again, but she nodded politely.

John Culpepper, Esquire

CHAPTER 9

1654, London

The turmoil in London had calmed down considerably since the family had escaped in 1650, but the first leather-skinned dockworker Alex spoke with gave him a wary look when he said his last name was Culpepper.

"Parliament is still looking for some Culpeppers," the man said. "Been searching for a Colonel Thomas Culpepper since the war ended. Said he's a traitor. They're offering a hefty reward to anyone who finds him, but they think he might have escaped the country. You wouldn't be related to him, would you?"

"Thomas Culpepper is dead," replied Alex dryly.

The dockworker narrowed his eyes for a moment and scrutinized Alex from head to toe. Finally, he shrugged and shuffled away to continue his work.

***

After two days of searching, Alex finally found a modest flat for his mother in downtown London, promising her he would look elsewhere for more suitable accommodations as time permitted. This was not the nature of lodgings she was accustomed to, but it was better than what they had when they first arrived in Virginia, and the best he could do for now.

Once she was settled in, he walked to the edge of town and hired a horse from the livery. He rode out to visit his aunt Cicely and aunt Frances. The two women hugged him like they hadn't seen him in years. He then realized they hadn't. The last time he'd seen his aunts was before the war when he was only ten. Except for the peppered graying of their hair and the lines around their eyes, the women looked the same as he remembered.

Aunt Cicely had been born in 1604, between his father and his uncle John. Aunt Frances was the youngest of the four siblings, born in 1608. Cicely had never married and was now an old spinster. He remembered his father telling him that before the war Aunt Cicely had lived alone in a flat in London with eight cats. He could picture her living like that. When the war broke out in 1642, she moved in with Frances north of the city. Alex was told it broke Aunt Cicely's heart to leave her cats behind, but she couldn't remain with them, living alone in the middle of a war. Aunt Frances was happy to take in her sister, but she refused the furry animals as they made her sneeze uncontrollably.

Alex also remembered hearing stories of Aunt Frances. When she was young, she was the talkative and bubbly sibling of the family, always the center of attention. She had married and moved to Middlesex when she was a teenager. The family didn't see much of her after that. She was an upper-class socialite, busy with her gatherings and functions, even during the roughest years of the war. She reminded Alex so much of his overbearing sister, who had been named after his aristocratic aunt.

When the war ended so horribly and John had to sneak the family out of the country, Alex's aunts were left behind. John and Thomas couldn't get to them in the short window of opportunity they had to escape. Frances's husband was not a royalist; in fact, he served in Parliament. He didn't participate in the fighting nor the execution of the king, but since Parliament had won the war, Thomas assured John that it would be safe for their sisters to stay behind in England.

The home Alex entered now was grand, certainly the finest residence he had seen in the last four years, and his aunts looked to be in good health, so it appeared his father had been correct.

"Alex, I'm so glad you came to visit. When did you get into town? Please come in.

Look at how you've grown! You look so much like your mother. We haven't seen you since you were a lad." Frances continued chatting about everything from the wall hangings to the recent weather. Apparently, Alex's father had also been correct about Aunt Frances being the centerpiece of every room.

Cicely laughed, rolled her eyes at her talkative sister, and smiled at Alex.

Aunt Frances, oblivious to the communication between the two, continued talking. "Alex, please come into the parlor and have a seat. I want to hear all about your voyage to Virginia. How are your siblings? How did you make your way back to England? Did John bring you? He still has a boat, right?"

Alex smiled. "All right, Aunt Frances. I'll tell you the whole story."

"If you can get a word in edgewise," Aunt Cicely whispered into his ear. She wrapped her arms around his elbow and they followed bouncing Frances into the well-appointed parlor.

"First of all, how are my brothers?" Frances said after she sat down.

"Aunt Frances, Aunt Cicely, that's actually the reason for my visit." Alex stood next to Cicely, looking down at Aunt Frances, holding his hat in his hands. "I'm afraid I have very sad news for you. My father was killed in Virginia."

Frances's hand flew to her mouth. Cicely's knees buckled and she landed on the sofa.

"I'm very sorry to deliver this bad news. I brought my mother back to England because she didn't want to remain in Virginia after my father's death."

"Katherine is here? Why didn't you bring her with you? Where is she staying?" Frances asked.

"She wasn't up to traveling today. I rented her a flat in town and she wishes to stay there for the time being."

"Oh, no, what about your siblings? Did they come back with you also?" Cicely asked.

"No, they stayed in Virginia. Uncle John found very respectable husbands for Anna and Frances, and JJ has been named the assistant surveyor general of the colony."

"Your sisters are married? I can't imagine how mature they are now. We haven't seen them since they were children." Frances patted the seat next to her. "Please sit down and tell us everything from the beginning. What happened to poor Thomas?"

Over the next few hours, Alex told the ladies the whole tale, from escaping England to his father's burial, nearly leaving Aunt Frances speechless, which was a rare thing.

Following the difficult and exhausting visit, Alex returned to his mother's flat and penned a letter to his uncle.

Dear Uncle John,

We have arrived safely and rented a flat in London. Mother is well and very happy to be home. I rode out to Aunt Frances's house today to deliver word of Father's death. She and Aunt Cicely were rightfully upset by the news, but they are both well and send their love. Please be advised that Parliament is still looking for royalists and the name Culpepper is at the top of their list. I don't think it wise for you to sail here at this time. I'm going to lie low myself for a while. I'll write to you again if and when circumstances change. Please give my regards to Aunt Mary, my cousins, and my siblings.

With warmest regards,
Alex Culpepper

CHAPTER 10

1656, France

JC arrived at the Château de Saint-Germain-en-Laye, just west of Paris, as the sun was beginning to set. He was greeted by the queen's guards and followed them across the sun-drenched grounds to the palace. They walked in the golden light along the gravel path between the rows and rows of formal gardens, fountains, and basins that lay in front of the symmetrical building, passing swans and peacocks that graced the well-manicured grounds. A multitude of archways lined the bottom floor of the palace's facade, and tall, thin windows lined the upper floors. It was the epitome of French flamboyance, more lavish than any home Queen Henrietta had ever occupied in England.

Upon entering the main hall, JC paused for a moment. In all his years serving the king, he had never seen a palace as excessive as this one. He was awed by the arched ceilings, marble statues, and extravagant decor. He followed the guards up the massive staircase, down a long corridor, and through the carved double doors that led into the queen's chambers. When he came before her, he bowed deeply.

"Lord Culpepper, it is so nice to see you again," she said warmly. "How is my son?"

"He is well, Your Majesty. His entourage is expected to arrive tomorrow."

"Why did you not wait to come with him?"

"I rode ahead to make sure his travels would be safe."

"I can't thank you enough for watching over him. Once we capture Cromwell and finally place my son on the throne, your loyalties will be richly rewarded."

JC bowed again. "Thank you, Your Majesty."

"You deserve anything your heart desires for protecting him as you have. You've been one of the most trustworthy supporters we've had."

"Thank you again, Your Majesty. Speaking of supporters, I've garnered enthusiastic support from our allies in Russia, and I've sent word to my son in Denmark to travel to The Hague and inform us immediately of the support of the nobles there."

Just before the king's execution, JC had taken Prince Charles from England for his own safety. They first traveled to Spain and eventually found their way to Denmark. Over the last few years, JC had been in negotiations with the Prince of Orange and the King of Denmark and had left his son, Thomas Culpepper, in charge of the talks as JC traveled to Russia to garner additional support. JC then made arrangements to move the prince to France at his mother's request.

Even though the prince's mother, Queen Henrietta, was the youngest daughter of King Henry IV of France and Marie de' Medici, she was not making much headway as far as getting her son on the throne. Many of the nobles were not happy with her marriage to King Charles I of England, and others did not want to battle the formidable English army now run by Oliver Cromwell. The exiled queen was forced to grovel at the feet of her nephew, the new king, Louis XIV, who was being less than helpful in the matter. She thought it prudent for her son to make an appearance before the French monarch and personally ask him for his vow of support. With pressure from surrounding countries and being reminded of the 1649 Scottish proclamation that Prince Charles was indeed King of England following his father's execution, France would eventually have to give its support. It didn't want to wage any kind of war on England, but it could surely help negotiate the boy onto the throne.

Following JC's visit with the queen, she offered him superb accommodations in the

French palace, asking him to remain with them and continue protecting the prince as he had promised the king he would do. JC obliged Her Majesty and prepared rooms for the prince's arrival.

JC enjoyed his own superb accommodations, but he missed his wife and children, who had remained in the Netherlands. There was no resolution to his desire to see them and probably never would be. His life was not centered around his family, it was always meant to be in the service of the crown. Since the king's execution, JC's new role as protector of the prince was ongoing, at least until the day he could be restored to the throne. If the royalists could raise an army, that day would come soon, but each monarch from each country seemed to play a game against the others, promising aide but being painfully slow to deliver. Each noble was concerned with keeping peace, causing sluggish negotiations. A member of each royal family was married off into another royal family, and one wouldn't want to be the cause of a feud with a neighbor, especially if that neighbor was married to one's sister or cousin. The prince's supporters worked tirelessly to raise an army, but the planning was slow moving and they struggled to keep their correspondence out of the hands of Cromwell's spies.

While JC traveled to Russia to garner support for the prince, his son Thomas continued talks with the royals of Denmark. A noble family by the name of Hesse promised to assist the royalists, stating it was anxious to see the Stuart family restored to the throne. Thomas, a stalwart young man who was now twenty-one, had traveled to The Hague to continue the slow-moving negotiations.

A month after JC arrived in France, he received a letter from Thomas stating that he had met with the royal family of Demark and with the Hesse family. They all confirmed they would offer their support. Thomas also mentioned in his letter that he was quite taken with a young woman in the Hesse family by the name of Margaretta. JC was thrilled with the news and hoped his son would marry a fine woman of good breeding and give him many grandchildren.

John Culpepper, Esquire

CHAPTER 11

1658, Katherine St. Leger Culpepper

My dearest uncle,

It is with great sadness that I pen this letter to you. I'm very sorry to inform you that my mother has passed away today after a quick but devastating illness. Katherine St. Leger Culpepper was the kindest and most beautiful woman I have ever known, inside and out. She will be greatly missed by everyone who knew her.

I'm very sorry for this sad news, Uncle. Please let Aunt Mary and my siblings know of the events and give the family my regards.

*Sincerely,
Your nephew,
Alex Culpepper*

John stood at the dock with the letter in his hands and looked up at the seabirds. "Why? Why would you take someone as good and kind as Katherine?" he murmured to the cloudy sky.

He turned and walked toward his horse. He stood next to it, not wanting to mount and go home to tell Mary. This would not be an easy task. Mary and Katherine had lived under the same roof for twenty years. They were like sisters.

When he arrived at the house, Mary was on the porch watching him approach. She took one look at his face and walked over to him as he climbed down from the mare.

"John? Is something wrong? What happened?"

John pulled the letter from his pocket and held it toward her. "It's from Alex."

"What? What happened?"

He exhaled. "Katherine is dead. Alex said she was ill."

Mary snatched the paper from his hand and unfolded it. As she read the letter, her free hand covered her lips. "Oh, no, we're going to have to tell JJ and the girls."

John walked toward the pasture, pulling his horse behind him. "I don't even know where JJ is."

Mary followed. "I'll ride with you to Anna's if you wish."

"That would be nice of you, dear. We'll go in the morning."

Later that evening, Mary sat on the sofa, staring blankly at the ashes piled high in the bottom of the fireplace.

John plopped down next to her. "What are you thinking, Mary?"

"I was thinking about how old we are. Our children are grown and never here. Even Johnny stays away with his brothers most of the time. Why would a fourteen-year-old want to stay away from home so much?"

"He's just a boy, doing what boys do. I lived at Middle Temple attending school when I wasn't much older than him."

"There were so many things we wanted to do with our lives, so many plans for our future, and the time is now gone. We are the last of our generation, you know. You and me and JC."

"I just turned fifty two. That means JC will be sixty this year. I remember us as boys, fishing at our grandfather's house. Thomas was there...Katherine was, too." He pouted. "We're certainly aging more quickly than I ever thought possible. Time has flown by."

Mary nodded and continued staring straight ahead, with lines of worry and sadness crossing her brow.

After a while, John broke the silence. "We've done the jobs we were meant to do, my dear. We've raised our children, we've looked after our family, we've buried our parents and our siblings. I guess this is the way life is supposed to be."

A tear ran down Mary's cheek. "I was hoping I would someday see her again."

"I know you were." He patted her knee. "Katherine will be deeply missed."

They sat in silence for a long time, lost in their own private thoughts.

John finally said, "Let's get to bed. We have to get on the road early in the morning to visit Anna. It's going to be a hard day for her."

CHAPTER 12

1658, Death of Oliver Cromwell

After nine years as Lord Protector of the Commonwealth of England, Oliver Cromwell took to his death bed. He had long suffered from symptoms of kidney stones and a bout of malaria worsened his condition. One of his daughters had died a few weeks earlier and the emotional strain seemed to hasten his decline.

At the age of fifty-nine, on Friday, September 3, 1658, Oliver Cromwell took his last breath. He was buried in an elaborate ceremony at Westminster Abbey, a formal observance rivaling the funeral of any monarch.

His intent was for his son, Richard, to succeed him as Lord Protector, but Richard had no political base in Parliament, so he was not readily accepted by its members as the leader of the Commonwealth. His protectorate lasted exactly nine months before he was forced to resign, and the Cromwell legacy was finished.

The English governor of Scotland, George Monck, stepped forward as a new leader and restored Parliament. Under his watchful eye and powerful presence, Parliament made the necessary constitutional adjustments to bring Prince Charles out of exile and place him on the throne. There were religious complications that needed to be discussed, as England was primarily Anglican, Scotland was mostly Presbyterian, and Ireland was predominantly Catholic, but with negotiations and long-needed tolerance, Parliament vowed it would see the prince on the throne by the turn of the decade.

After the prince's men entered the negotiations, the discussions became more intense when it came to the fate that should befall the traitors who had led the revolution that resulted in the king's death. Some men would survive, many would not. Only the prince and Parliament would be able to negotiate which ones would be which.

The members of Parliament postdated all the paperwork and laws, claiming the prince to be King Charles II and the rightful heir to the throne since his father's death in 1649. They acted as if the last decade had never happened. JC gathered his family and men in celebration and began planning the king's triumphant return to London.

CHAPTER 13

1659, Lancaster County, Virginia

John met with the Virginia General Assembly in Jamestown every day for an entire week, where as an experienced lawyer, he oversaw their debates of deciding how to divide the tithes in each county. After all of the members of the assembly argued in the stifling heat of the room for hours and hours, they finally signed the final agreement, dividing the money for roads, docks, and local militias.

After the proceedings were finished, John headed north to visit Henry. At times he wondered if he would make it. It was so hot, it was even hard to breathe, and the sweltering heat made everything sticky. John didn't remember it ever being this hot in Virginia, and the humid nights didn't offer much relief. Tree birds ceased their songs as they were trying to conserve enough energy to stay cool, but the blaring night sounds of the katydids and tree frogs made up for the daytime silence. Their songs were the loudest John had ever heard. He spent the night under the stars not far from Henry's house, arriving too late to barge in. He stared into the tree tops, wondering if he would ever fall asleep with the noise. Eventually, he did, and he awoke with the sunrise, covered in a gloss of sweat. He wiped his brow with a handkerchief and rode straight to Henry's.

They hadn't seen each other more than once or twice a year since Henry moved away from home seven years earlier, but John had heard rumors that Henry was considering a move to Portsmouth in Lower Norfolk County, and also that he had a serious relationship with his friend Bill Greene's younger sister, Elizabeth. John promised Mary he would go up and find out what was going on. He did so under the premise of his wife's desires, but he was more than a little curious himself.

"Father! What brings you all the way up here?" Henry exclaimed when he found John at his doorstep.

"I promised your mother I'd come up and check on you."

"Come in. Let me get you something cool to drink."

John entered the home and found the accommodations quite comfortable, filled with more amenities than the last time he had visited a year or so ago.

"Have a seat at the table. Are you

hungry? I'll put on some eggs," Henry offered.

"That sounds good." John looked around. "You've done a lot with this place. It looks very…um…homey."

"That's thanks to Elizabeth. She's been helping me with the house. Apparently I didn't know how to turn a house into a home, but she's put her touches in all the right places. She's been a great help."

"I heard rumors about you and Elizabeth. She's your partner's sister, right?"

"Yes, she's Bill's younger sister."

At that moment, the door opened between the parlor and the back of the house where the bedrooms were, and a pretty girl with long, disheveled curls entered. She was dressed in a thin gown and house slippers, and she stopped in her tracks when she saw John sitting at the table.

"There she is now. Elizabeth, I'd like you to meet my father. This is John Culpepper."

John stood and smiled at the young lady who had obviously just risen from bed. Her face blushed a deep crimson.

He reached for her hand. "It's very nice to make your acquaintance, young lady."

"And yours, Mr. Culpepper."

John held her hand and looked at her for a minute, taking in her loveliness and wondering why she was sleeping at his son's house. Henry interrupted the thoughts.

"Would you like some eggs, Elizabeth?"

"Um, yes, but I should dress first. I didn't realize we had company. I'll be back in a few minutes." She nearly ran back through the doorway she had entered.

John looked at his son. "We?"

"Excuse me?" Henry said.

"She said she didn't realize 'we' had company."

"Yes, Father." Henry placed a cup of cider in front of his father as he sat back down at the table. "I was going to send you word that Elizabeth and I married last week. I was trying to find some time to take her to Accomac to meet you and Mother, but I've been so busy with the plantation and the move."

"I wish you would have told us before you got married. I'm sure your mother would have wanted to be there."

"I know she would have, and I'm sorry, but I didn't want to wait until the family could be together. When that beautiful girl agreed to marry me, I wanted to do so right away before she changed her mind." Henry chuckled as he set two more cups of cider on the table. He sat down and took a drink.

"Elizabeth is a lovely girl. Your mother will be pleased." John grinned at his son, the first of his children to marry. He had a flash of Henry's future with a lovely woman by his side and raising a fine family, and he hoped Henry would be a better father than he was. "I'm very happy for you."

"Thank you, Father. We're very happy together."

"That's obvious. Now, what about this move you're planning?"

"We're going to Portsmouth. I've secured some land and a house there."

"Your mother will be pleased. That's a lot closer to our house."

Henry nodded as Elizabeth reentered and took a seat at the table.

"So, Elizabeth, tell me all about yourself so I can report back to my wife," John said.

John Culpepper, Esquire

CHAPTER 14

1659, London

As Prince Charles's messengers negotiated with Parliament the details of his ascent to the throne, JC returned to London to make plans to bring the king home. It had been nearly a decade since JC had stepped foot on the soil of his homeland, and he was delighted. He made the rounds, visiting people he hadn't seen in a long time, and eventually went to a small flat in London to see his cousin Alex.

"Welcome home, JC. It's nice to see you back in England," Alex said.

"It's good to be home. I was very sorry to hear about your mother. She was a lovely woman."

"Thank you, cousin. I miss her greatly. With my siblings living in Virginia and all of the Culpeppers scattered throughout the world, it's been a mite lonely around here."

"What about your aunts?"

"They're in Middlesex. I don't see them very often."

"When you do, give them my regards. I haven't seen them in decades."

"I certainly will. So, tell me, when will you escort King Charles to England?"

"We're going to wait until spring. We're organization the grandest procession and coronation the country has ever seen. Parliament has already signed a document naming Charles as the true and rightful king from the moment of his father's death. It's like Cromwell never even existed."

Alex grimaced. "Cromwell was a devious bastard. He nearly ruined this country. The way I see it, not only did our family lose everything because of him, but my father died in Virginia because of him."

"Well, he's gone now, and I will do my best to retrieve the family's lands as soon as we see Charles sitting on the throne, as he was always meant to."

"If there's anything I can do to help you plan his homecoming, just let me know."

"Actually, there is one thing you can do. The king has given me back the title to Leeds Castle, and I'm going to offer it to my son Thomas and his new wife. When they come home from the Netherlands, I would like to ask you to be at the castle to greet them for me. I won't have the time to go to them since I have to be with the king."

"I didn't know Thomas married. Who is his bride?"

"Her name is Margaretta van Hesse. I haven't met her myself, but I know of the Hesse family and they are nobles with quite a fortune. I don't know how Thomas is going to keep her in the style she is accustomed to."

"They're going to live at Leeds?"

"That's what I came over to talk to you about. As you know, after your father died, Leeds Castle reverted to my ownership. It was quickly lost to the Commonwealth, but since the king has had it restored to me, I was wondering if you would consider moving there and overseeing the estate."

"I would be very happy to do that," Alex said.

"My son will undoubtedly have much work to do in the service of the king, and Margaretta, not being familiar with English customs will be in need of new friends. I'm sure she would love to have someone her own age living in the house to help her adjust to our country."

"She's young?"

"Yes, she's in her mid-twenties."

"I would be happy to befriend her. Let me know when I can move in."

"You can move in right away. They'll arrive prior to the king's procession, so I don't see why you couldn't go and get the house ready now."

"I'll go to Leeds Castle right away and have it livable by the time Thomas and Margaretta arrive. Have you heard from Uncle John?"

"Not lately, but I need to write to him and tell him of the king's coronation plans."

"Tell him I heard Edmund Plowden died last month in London. Apparently he returned to England following my father's death and has been living in hiding until now. His last wish was to be buried in his native parish churchyard in Salop, but his wife had him buried in unfamiliar grounds at St. Clement's in London. Uncle John will be extremely pleased by that news."

"Plowden? The man suspected in your father's death?"

Alex nodded.

"I'll send a letter to John right away."

CHAPTER 15

1659, Margaretta van Hesse

On an unusually warm September afternoon, Alex heard horses' hooves and grinding wagon wheels crossing the drawbridge into the courtyard of Leeds Castle. He ran outside to see if Thomas and Margaretta had arrived. He emerged through the stone archway as four ornate carriages pulled by beautiful, brown Dartmoor horses came to a halt in the courtyard. The horses whinnied as the doors of the first three carriages opened simultaneously and servants emerged in a flurry of activity. A footman opened the door of the fourth carriage and held out his hand to assist its passenger in disembarking. That's when Alex saw her.

She floated down the carriage step like a cool breeze on a sweltering day, adorned in satin and lace, dark brown curls resting on her slender shoulders. A servant opened a parasol and held it over her head to shield her from the sun as she bent and smoothed out her crumpled skirt. She stood up straight and looked around the courtyard. Her face was that of an angel's. When her green eyes fell to Alex, she smiled. He felt as if his heart skipped a beat. Thomas Culpepper emerged from the carriage next and glanced at her. He followed her gaze and noticed Alex standing near the doorway.

"Oh, you must be Alex! My father said you readied the house for us," said Thomas as he approached Alex and shook his hand.

"Yes, I did. It's nice to see you, Lord Thomas."

Thomas slapped Alex on the shoulder. "I'd like to extend my sincerest thanks for your service. After all, you're not even a servant. We're family. I'm not sure how, but my father tells me we're cousins."

"Our grandfathers were brothers."

"Oh, yes, that's it. Well, Alex, I'd like you to meet my wife, Lady Margaretta." Thomas walked back toward the carriage and Alex followed. Thomas took his wife's gloved hand and pulled her rather roughly toward Alex.

Thomas released her hand, and the woman smiled at Alex as she removed her glove. Alex nodded to her. "Lady Culpepper, it is a pleasure to make your acquaintance." Alex took her fingertips and brushed his lips across her knuckles.

She didn't say a word, but her eyes were warm and her smile was affectionate.

Thomas leaned toward Alex. "She doesn't talk much, but that's good, right? Don't want a wife who yaps all the time. Truthfully, she probably doesn't want you to hear her Danish accent. It's very silly sounding." Thomas laughed at his wife's expense. He then turned and barked orders to his drivers and footmen to unload the three carriages, stating that Alex would show them where to place the items. He marched toward the back wagon and yelled something at one of the servants.

"I'm very pleased to meet you, Alex," Margaretta said with the most charming accent, a mix between French and Dutch.

"And I you, Lady Culpepper. Welcome to England and to Leeds Castle." Alex gestured around the courtyard. "I hope you'll be very happy here, and I will be pleased to remain at your service as long as you need me," Alex said.

"It's quite beautiful, and please, call me Margaretta."

Alex nodded.

"Alex, I need you to show my wife to her chambers and let the drivers know where to put our belongings." Thomas removed his hat and ran his fingers through his curly hair. "We've had somewhat of a long journey and I'm sure my wife is quite fatigued. Do we have any wine or ale on the premises?"

"Certainly. I'll show m'lady to her room and meet you in the dining room with some refreshments." He offered Margaretta his arm and led her into the castle. Over his shoulder, he heard Thomas barking more orders at his staff. He wondered how such a buffoon ever attracted the affections of someone as beautiful and refined as Margaretta van Hesse.

Early the next morning, Thomas knocked on Alex's chamber door and Alex answered in only his nightshirt. "Lord Thomas, what can I do for you?"

"I just wanted to tell you I'll be going into London for a while, so please make sure my wife is comfortable."

"Oh, of course. I'll see to it."

Thomas stomped down the dim hall toward the staircase.

"When will you be returning?" Alex called after him.

"I'm not sure, but please do as I asked," Thomas said over his shoulder without breaking stride.

"Certainly."

Over the next few weeks, Alex spent many hours with Lady Margaretta, learning of her family's vast wealth and her husband's suspected roaming eye. Alex couldn't believe anyone would neglect a woman the way Thomas seemed to neglect Margaretta, but since he had gone into London, he hadn't returned to the castle even once to check on her. He seemed to have abandoned her in a house in a country where she knew no one.

It grew painfully obvious to Alex that

Thomas married Margaretta only for her money. Margaretta didn't come right out and say she knew the truth about her husband, but she hinted at it. If she didn't realize the truth, Alex would not be the one to tell her. He would, however, make sure she didn't become lonely. She had arrived with no ladies-in-waiting, no chambermaids, not one female to assist her in becoming familiar with her surroundings. The only servants who arrived with her and Thomas were the cook and a few drivers and footmen who were not much more than boys.

Alex would need to hire more staff.

John Culpepper, Esquire

CHAPTER 16

1660, Margaretta and Alex

Alex had spent a vast amount of money staffing the castle and thought Margaretta was settling in nicely, but about two months after her arrival he found her sitting in one of the reception rooms in front of the roaring fireplace, sobbing.

"What is wrong, Margaretta?"

She sniffled and dried her face with a handkerchief. "I'm feeling a little dejected. I'm sorry for you to see me like this, Alex."

Alex sat in the chair across from her and leaned forward, his elbows resting on his knees. "Oh, my dear, don't be sorry." He reached for her hands. "I don't want you to be sad." He looked into her eyes and his heart almost burst from seeing the pain in her emerald eyes. "What can I do to bring a smile back to your face?"

She looked away. "I'm afraid there's nothing you can do."

"Nonsense. There has to be something that will stop these tears. Do you like your new chambermaids?"

"Yes, it's not that."

"Is the kitchen servant to your liking?"

She nodded.

"Then what is it, my dear? What can I do for you?"

"There's nothing you can do." She wiped her tears and sighed. "Since I was a little girl, I had hoped to live a wonderful life with a wonderful man, a man who loved me. I wanted to create a happy family with many children. I wanted to feel special and be a good mother and wife."

Alex didn't know what to say, so he remained silent. He knew she would never have that life with a man like Thomas Culpepper.

"One of my servants let it slip that my husband has not returned home these last few months because he is living in London with a mistress."

"A mistress?"

"Her name is Susannah Willis."

"I've never heard of her, but it's certainly not unusual for men in this country to take a mistress. It doesn't mean he doesn't love you."

"If he loved me he'd give me a child. Since our wedding night, he has not touched me, but he apparently touches this Susannah Willis."

"Oh, Margaretta, I'm so sorry you're feeling this way. I'll tell you what, I'll go down to the cellar and bring up some wine and we'll have our own celebration."

"What is there to celebrate? The fact that my husband loves another woman?"

Alex slipped off his chair and fell to his knees in front of her. "No, you should celebrate the fact that you *are* loved."

Her forehead creased in confusion.

He was tempted to tell her how much he cared for her, but restrained himself. "You are very loved, Margaretta. I care for you a great deal, more than you know, and I shall remain by your side as your greatest friend and confidant."

She looked surprised for a moment, then a small smile formed on her lips. "I don't know what I'd do in this strange country without you. No one here speaks like I do and the ladies don't dress the way I do."

"Well, we can fix one of those issues. How about we go into London tomorrow and do some shopping? We'll find the latest baubles and finery and hire someone to design a new wardrobe for you."

"Do you think my husband will return then?"

Alex looked down at the floor so she wouldn't see the truth in his eyes. "Honestly, I don't know the answer to that, but it will make you feel better, will it not?"

"Yes. Yes, it will make me feel better."

"Good. I'll go get that wine and I'll return in a few minutes."

CHAPTER 17

Spring 1660, Governor Berkeley

Even before the restored king returned to England, he began replacing Cromwell's appointments with men he respected and trusted.

John heard a horse approach one day and emerged from the house to greet his visitor.

"Will! Nice to see you. What brings you out here?"

Will Berkeley stepped down from his horse and reached for John's hand. "I have some wonderful news. King Charles has granted the governorship of Virginia back to me."

"That is wonderful news."

Berkeley pulled a letter from his breast pocket. "I also picked this up for you in Jamestown. The dockmaster said it was delivered a few days ago from London."

John flipped the letter over and saw the

seal of his cousin JC. He looked back at Berkeley. "The last time I got a letter from JC, it said the war had just begun. JC generally doesn't write to me, so I hope it's not bad news again." John snapped the seal and unfolded the crisp paper.

My dear cousin,

I have returned to England to prepare for the king's arrival. Everyone is excited beyond measure, except for the traitors who revolted against him. He pardoned many of them, but there are quite a few being held in the Tower awaiting his arrival and punishment. You may not be happy to hear that he pardoned General Thomas Fairfax. I know the general and Uncle Alexander had many battles and I know Thomas ran into him on more than one occasion, but I assume the king would like to put the horrible incidents of the past in the past and he thinks he may be able to use Fairfax's talents in the future.

I also spoke with Alex. My son Thomas and his new bride are returning to England, and since Leeds Castle is now in my possession, I offered it to my son and asked Alex to oversee the estate. He was happy to do so, and everything is going well.

I am penning this letter as a favor to Alex. He asked me to tell you Sir Edmund Plowden has died in London. I didn't hear any more details of his death, but I sincerely hope it was in a bloody duel and someone had the pleasure of killing the scoundrel. Apparently his last will requested that he be buried at his home parish cemetery, but his wife had him buried in unfamiliar grounds. I don't blame her for being spiteful. That man all but ruined her life, not to mention yours.

I must close for now and see to the king's business. I will be residing at Whitehall Palace for the time being if you need me, and Alex will be staying at Leeds Castle indefinitely. Please give my love to Mary and I will write again after the coronation has taken place. Long live the king!

Sincerely,
JC

John laughed out loud.

"What does it say?" asked Berkeley.

"Plowden's dead!" John handed his friend the letter and waited for him to read it.

"Looks like Mabel Plowden had the last laugh," Berkeley said.

"I wish we could have tried him for Thomas's murder, but it looks like Plowden in death will pay the ultimate price for being the rake that he was in life."

"I also wish we could have found those brothers Plowden hired. Last I heard they were seen in New Albion, but without my powers as governor, I couldn't do anything about arresting them and transporting them down here. Perhaps that should be the first thing on my agenda."

John shook his head. "It doesn't much matter now, Will. Plowden's dead and he was the cause of my brother's death. Those other two were just drunkards who tagged along."

"If you think it best to let it go, I will, but if you change your mind, you let me know and I'll see what I can do. Being governor opens a lot of doors that have long been closed."

CHAPTER 18

May 29, 1660, The King Takes the Throne

On the very day of Charles Stuart's thirtieth birthday, he entered the gates of London as Charles the Second, King of England, Scotland, and Ireland. His procession marched through the streets of London and was indeed the grandest jubilee the city had ever seen. Every citizen, young and old, lined the cobblestone streets, tossing flowers and cheering at the spectacle. Drummers and flutists marched in unison, filling the air with a grand and happy tune. Horses, hundreds of them, wore new plate on their faces and chests, and richly colored velvet across their backs. They pranced as if the parade and massive crowd were for their own enjoyment. Their riders—barons, earls, and courtiers, most of whom had been exiled and now reinstated to their former status—were wearing their finest garments and bejeweled with every expensive bauble the new king had bestowed upon them.

Following a lengthy procession, trumpets with banners flowing from their long pipes shouted the announcement of the king's imminent arrival. The cheer of the crowd grew to a fevered pitch as a knight hoisting the king's standard trotted before them. JC rode behind the knight, and following JC was the king, his white horse covered by a sapphire blanket. The king was dressed all in white. His dark hair fluttered in the afternoon breeze, and his lanky frame, at over six feet tall, made him visible to all. He was like a god appearing before his people. The men bowed deeply while the women curtsied and tossed flowers on the ground before his horse. The king waved and smiled at his onlookers. They cheered louder. The king was followed by his sergeant at arms, his large armored cavalry, and a sampling of his foot soldiers — an army of hundreds. Following the army, subordinates walked, offering alms to the citizens in attendance. Gold, silver, jewelry, coins. The horde gathered up the trinkets like starving birds fighting over crusts of bread. The king knew his people hadn't received anything of worth from the dastardly Cromwell, and he was determined to have his people love him. They could be bought with fear as Cromwell had done, but it was easier to buy them with treasure. Many members of the crowd fell in behind the procession, following it toward

Whitehall Palace, hoping to see and receive more. Others left the extravaganza and returned to their homes.

No one in the lengthy procession was happier or prouder than JC, who rode tall on his mount with an enormous smile across his face. JC had protected the heir to the throne for more than a decade, hoping and praying this day would come. He had done his job well. The Culpepper family was on the verge of reaping the rewards it so richly deserved. The king made sure the title to Leeds Castle was free and clear and belonged to JC in whole, and as soon as the festivities were over, JC planned to ask the king to restore all the lands and homes that had previously belonged to the family. He would even ask for land in Virginia so his cousin, John, could live in the style Culpeppers were meant to.

* * *

A few weeks after the procession, Alex received a message from JC to come to Sir Edward Ford's house in London at once. The letter didn't say why, but Alex had already heard that the joy of the restoration had been clouded by a smallpox epidemic raging through London, taking the lives of the king's younger brother Henry and sister Mary. Alex assumed JC wished to speak with him about Leeds Castle or other family business or perhaps the king's business, but he didn't know why they would conduct such business at JC's friend's estate.

When Alex arrived, he was not expecting to be greeted by the house's servants and escorted up the stairs to the sleeping chambers. When the door swung open and he saw JC lying pale in a large bed, he understood.

"Cousin! I didn't know you were ill," Alex said as he neared JC's bedside. "I would have hurried even more."

JC waved his hand, dismissing Alex's comment. "You're here now."

"Yes, I am. What can I do for you?"

"I need to get my will in order."

"Your will? Surely you're not that ill."

"I'm afraid I am. I have the king's word that our family manors and lands will be restored. I want you to help me write my will to make sure my estate is taken care of, and I want you to write a letter to John to tell him of the good news, both of the restoration and the impending reinstatement of the family's wealth."

A few weeks earlier, JC had spoken with the king, who promised to grant the family everything JC had wished, including sizable land grants in the colonies of Virginia and Carolina. After forty years in the service of the monarchy, living in exile with the king for the last ten, JC had seen to it that the Culpepper family finally returned to the aristocracy. After Alex penned the letter to John, he asked JC if they should summon his son Thomas to help write the will.

"I've already sent word to him that I am dying. He hasn't responded." A look of sadness crossed his face.

"Should I go fetch him?" Alex asked.

JC shook his head. "There's no time."

Alex wasn't surprised that Thomas neglected his father just as he had always neglected his wife. The man was truly the most self-centered character ever to grace the streets of London.

On July 3, 1660, only weeks after his triumphant return to the city with the restored king, JC dictated his last will. Alex sat next to the bed, his shaky hand moving across the page as JC spoke softly and slowly.

"Being of sound mind, I declare this the last will and testament of John, Lord Culpepper, Baron of Thoresway. I wish to be buried in the vault which my father, Sir Thomas Culpepper, Knight, hath built in Hollingbourne.

"Whereas His Majesty in answer to my petition of June 27 last hath engaged his royal word for payment out of his first receipts for clearing of my paternal estate and towards paying portions to my younger children.

"To my daughter Elizabeth, four thousand pounds as she will release her right of manors and lands of Greenway Court.

"To my daughter Judith, five hundred pounds at her marriage to be overseen by her sister Elizabeth, and one thousand five hundred pounds out of His Majesty's debt.

"To my son John, five hundred pounds, and his elder brother Thomas as his guardian until the age of twenty-one.

"To my son Cheney, five hundred pounds, and his elder brother Thomas as this guardian until the age of twenty-one.

"To my son Francis, one thousand pounds at the age of twenty one.

"To my daughter Philippa, five hundred pounds, and her elder brother Thomas to educate her until the age of eighteen.

"To my servant John Rowe for care of me in my sickness, one hundred twenty pounds.

"To Sir Edward Ford in whose house I now lie, two hundred pounds for his trouble.

"I beg His Majesty towards redeeming of my distressed family and estate from ruin. His Majesty will take order with his court that the whole debt of twelve thousand pounds be punctually paid to my executor.

"My eldest son and heir Thomas to be executor. I leave all of my real estate to my eldest son and all future lands and manors which will be returned to the family."

Alex wrote feverishly, but stopped at the mention of Thomas as heir. Surely JC should choose someone else. Thomas didn't even have the decency to be here with his dying father.

"Pen it how I have said," JC said, seemingly reading Alex's mind. "Thomas is my eldest and will be given all that I have to give."

Alex shrugged and continued writing. When he finished, he held the writing tablet in front of JC and placed the quill in his shaky hand. JC squinted at the document as Alex pointed at the bottom, and JC scrawled his signature.

Alex remained at JC's side every day and night until JC took his last breath on July 11, 1660.

A few weeks later, Alex traveled to Westminster Hall to witness the probate of JC's will. Lord Thomas, nearly the sole heir of JC's life of service to the monarchy, and now officially the second baron of Thoresway, never made an appearance.

Lori Crane

CHAPTER 19

January 30, 1661, Posthumous Execution

The new king granted amnesty to all but fifty of Cromwell's former supporters. Some of the fifty were punished by life in prison; others were excluded from holding public office for the remainder of their lives. Nine of the fifty — the ones who signed the former king's death warrant — were hanged, drawn, and quartered.

The body of John Bradshaw, who had presided over the court at the time of King Charles I's trial and execution, was exhumed to suffer the indignity of a posthumous decapitation. He wasn't the only one.

On the twelfth anniversary of King Charles I's execution, the new king had Oliver Cromwell's rotting corpse exhumed from Westminster Abbey. The king's men paraded the appalling carcass through the streets of London and hanged it in chains at Tyburn. The next day,

Cromwell's head was severed and put on display on a stake outside Westminster Hall.

"How long would Your Majesty desire Cromwell's head to remain on the stake?" asked the king's sergeant at arms.

"Forever!" replied the king. "It will remain as a symbol of what happens to men who turn against the throne."

As the king wished, the rotting head of Oliver Cromwell remained on exhibition, a spectacle that drew enormous crowds.

CHAPTER 20

1661, Susannah Willis

Margaretta climbed down from the carriage with Alex's assistance. She stepped onto the cobblestone street and looked around in awe. No matter how many times he brought her into town, the bustling streets always took her breath away. Merchants moved their wares in carts, boys ran past them followed by barking mongrels, women appeared from second-story windows, hanging their wash from ropes tied across the upper floors of the street. There were so many people in such a small place. After Alex sent the driver away with instructions to return in one hour, he guided Margaretta across the street to her favorite boutique. While walking in the middle of the street, they narrowly avoided a peddler pushing a cart of vegetables. It bounced across the rough cobblestone.

"Watch yourself," he said to Margaretta as he pulled he out of the way of the oncoming cart.

She smiled at his chivalry.

The boutique before them carried a wide array of imported silks and satins from the Orient and the latest laces and jewels from France.

"I hope you find many fabrics and trinkets to your liking today," he said.

"I'm sure I will," she said as he pushed open the door for her. A brass bell announced their arrival.

"Would you like me to accompany you into the shop or would you like to shop alone?" he asked.

She looked around the shop and saw only one other woman and decided to not put Alex through the humiliation of standing next to her while she looked through laces and baubles. "I'll be fine if you would like to go and do something else."

"I have nothing else to do and am at your service for the entire day. But, I'll remain outside and give you some time to shop."

He held the door open for her and she entered the boutique without him. She walked to the middle of the shop and turned back to see him standing outside of the shop's large window. He looked inside and smiled at her. Comforted by the fact that he was near, she turned her attention to the rows of tables stacked high with the most beautiful fabrics she had ever seen. She walked to the nearest table and reached down to touch a pale blue silk at the same time as the other woman in the store began to pick it up. Their hands grazed each other's and Margaretta quickly drew her hand back and looked up at the woman. She smiled and excused herself, but the blonde woman remained frozen, staring at her.

"My apologies, madam. Please excuse me," Margaretta repeated.

The woman dropped the fabric and hurried toward the exit, struggling with the heavy door in what looked like an attempt to escape. The woman was dressed in the finest fabrics sewn into the latest fashions, but there was something very lowly about her, almost pauper-like. Her unkempt hair was tangled up in her lace collar, her nails not manicured. Margaretta looked toward the front window for the reassurance of Alex's presence and saw Alex's face turn immediately pale at the sight of the woman exiting the store. Margaretta watched him turn away as his eyes followed the woman's movements. The woman ran across the cobblestone street and straight into the arms of Margaretta's husband. Thomas wrapped the woman in his arms as she began to cry. Instantly, Margaretta knew who this woman was—her husband's mistress, his whore. This was Susannah Willis. Margaretta hurried outside, but Alex met her on the other side of the door and tried to stop her. She pushed past him.

"Thomas?" Margaretta said, marching

across the cobblestone with Alex trailing behind.

Thomas didn't reply, but his face turned pale. He looked at Alex over Margaretta's shoulder and nodded.

Alex nodded back.

Margaretta glanced back and forth between the men, not being able to read their expressions.

Without a word, Thomas grabbed Susannah Willis by the elbow and escorted her away, leaving Margaretta and Alex standing on the street outside the fabric shop.

* * *

Alex and Margaretta rode back to Leeds Castle in silence. He didn't know what to say to her. He was finally helping her feel better, finally bringing the rose back to her cheeks, and now his efforts were thwarted. By the look on her face, she had reverted to the gloomy mood she was in immediately following her arrival in England. As they neared the castle, he finally spoke. "Margaretta, I know you're upset. I would be, too, but—"

"I'm not upset. I'm angry," she interrupted him. "I'm angrier than I've ever been in my whole life." She was about to release all of the anger and pain she had suffered the last few months. She knew it wasn't the proper thing to do, but she hoped Alex would remain silent and give her the space to be cross. "How dare he show her off around London! I suppose she attends every royal event there is to attend while I sit alone in the country without a husband. I'm not a naïve woman. I never expected a marriage based upon money to become one of love, but I at least thought a man with the esteemed name of Culpepper would show me a shred of respect and decency. I don't want to feel sorry for myself because my clothing is not the latest styles and then run into my husband's mistress in all her finery. She looked like a sow someone tried to make presentable. No matter how much finery you put on the thing, it's still a sow."

Alex laughed out loud.

Margaretta realized how silly the idea was and laughed, too.

"Margaretta, I love you," Alex blurted out.

She stopped laughing and turned to him. "What?" she asked.

He was as surprised as she when the words came out of his mouth. The horses were crossing the drawbridge and he knew if he was going to admit his feelings for her, it would have to be quickly. When the carriage bumped onto the hard ground on the other side of the bridge and came to a stop in the courtyard, the driver would be opening the door.

Alex breathed in deeply. "There. I've said it. I've loved you since the moment you stepped down from the carriage the day you arrived, and I've grown to love you more and more with each passing day I've had the pleasure to know you. I'm glad you're not sad after seeing Susannah Willis. I'm happy that you're angry. It makes me laugh. And I'm glad Thomas hasn't been here. He's not the most upstanding example of the men in the Culpepper family, and I'm afraid I wouldn't be able to stomach seeing you with him."

Her surprised expression did not change.

The carriage stopped and he heard the driver's boots headed toward the door. At this moment, he didn't care if they were seen. He traced the curve of Margaretta's cheek with his finger. She didn't back away. He moved toward her and kissed her gently on the lips. She kissed him back. He hesitated, not wanting to be the first to pull away. She didn't pull away, either, and their kiss lingered as the carriage door handle turned and bright sunlight entered the cool interior.

The driver stood to the side of the opened door, not looking into the carriage, only waiting to help Margaretta down. Alex rose, exited the carriage, and stepped in front of him, offered his own hand to Margaretta. She emerged from the carriage with a smile on her face, and they strolled into the castle, still holding hands.

John Culpepper, Esquire

CHAPTER 21

1663, The Culpepper

"How long will you be gone?" Mary asked, concentrating on the dirty breakfast dishes before her.

"Only a few days. I promised James that I would join him on one of his surveying jobs, so we're heading down to Portsmouth." John reached around her and placed his cup in the washbasin.

"I wish you would have told me. I just pulled a bunch of vegetables from the garden. I won't be able to eat them all myself."

"I'm sorry. I guess it slipped my mind."

"Does this have anything to do with Henry? He said he was coming up from Portsmouth in a few weeks and then said something I didn't understand about sailing to England?"

John didn't answer. He turned and walked back to the table.

She turned to look at him. "John?"

He sighed and nodded, not wanting to meet her gaze.

"Sailing to England?!" she said, more of a statement than a question. "When were you going to tell me this?"

"It's not yet planned. That's why we're going to Portsmouth today."

Her brow creased. "So, it's not a surveying job?"

"No, it's not. I didn't want to worry you needlessly, but James and I are going to Portsmouth to see about a ship."

Mary placed her hands on her hips. "What ship? The *Thomas and John* was dry docked years ago."

John looked down at the table, feeling like a child in trouble, and he spoke softly and slowly. "I, um, we're going to provision our new ship."

"What new ship?"

He looked at her. Her face was three shades of red. She was livid and he wondered how much he should tell her. "The boys and I have been discussing this for quite some time. Robbie and Denny have the urge to sail. I can't deny them that. And James is a grown man now. He wants to run his own business. So...," he sighed, "I bought a new ship. It's larger than my last one. I'm thinking of naming it the *Culpepper*." He smiled tentatively.

He could see her anger bubbling to the

surface by the way she was wringing her hands. Before she had the chance to start screaming at him, he continued, "I'm sorry to be so secretive, but sitting in Virginia and playing the role of lawyer is slowly sucking the life out of me. The boys are interested in sailing and who better to teach them than me?"

She didn't move, but the anger in her face softened to concern. "Our sons want to sail?"

He nodded. "And I am more than please to get back on the sea myself."

"I admit I like to see this spark back in your eyes, but John, you're not just talking about leaving the family for a few months, you're talking about putting our children's welfare in jeopardy. You haven't sailed for thirteen years. Are you sure it's safe?"

"To sail or be seen in England?"

"Both."

John rose and reached for her hands. "Yes, my dear, it is safe on both accounts. I remember how to command a ship, and Alex wrote that England is back to normal since King Charles took the throne. I want to return to London and see if we can reestablish our merchant business there. Remember how lucrative it was? I think we could do that again. James said he wants to run his own business and would be happy to stay in London and oversee things on that end."

"James is just a boy."

"James is not a boy. He's twenty-four

years old, Mary. He's more than capable of living on his own and running a business."

"What about Denny and Robbie?"

"They don't want to stay in London, but they are interested in learning to sail. We'll see how they do on the voyage, and if all goes well, perhaps I'll set them up with their own trading route with ports of call here and London, and maybe even Barbados."

Tears came to her eyes. "Barbados? You're taking *all* my boys to London and Barbados? At least the last time you sailed, I had Katherine by my side. I don't have anyone now. I can't believe you would leave me here all alone."

"You won't be alone. Johnny is still here."

She rolled her eyes. "Johnny is never here. He hasn't been home in months. He stays down in Albemarle half the time and runs around with those troublemakers over in Jamestown the other half."

"They're not troublemakers. They consider themselves independents. They only want to decrease our reliance on the crown. We live on the other side of the world but still rely on England for assistance. We don't get much, but they tax us like there's no tomorrow."

"I just hope those boys never cause enough trouble to be charged with anything. I'd hate to see Johnny in court for doing something wrong, something we both know he was probably cajoled into by those other boys."

"I don't think they have to twist Johnny's arm very hard. He has a rebel streak in him. I wouldn't be surprised if he was the one doing the cajoling. Besides, the king is too busy trying to put England back together and surely doesn't have time to worry about some rebellious boys in some distant colony. He knows we can take care of our own."

"Still, Johnny worries me to death. Someday that boy is going to cross the line and find himself in a heap of trouble."

"Maybe I should send Henry to find him so we can take him with us, then."

"That's probably a good idea." Mary turned back to her dishes. "I can't believe I just said that."

* * *

A few months later, Mary stood alone on the dock as her five sons and husband raised the sails on the *Culpepper*. She wiped tears from her cheeks in between waving farewell.

"Mother looks so sad," Henry said, after the ship went around the bend and Mary disappeared from sight.

"Henry, my boy, I have sailed across the ocean dozens and dozens of times, leaving your mother standing on the dock with that same expression on her face. She'll be fine. You need to keep your mind on your job. A ship is no place to become melancholy or to let your mind wander. There are too many things that can go wrong and too many ways you can get injured." He looked down at a rope an inch from Henry's foot as a sailor on the yardarm was raising a sail. The rope quickly uncoiled and traveled upward. John pointed down. "See? If you were on the other side of that rope, you could have been knocked down. Don't worry about your mother. She's a strong woman. Stronger than any other person I've ever known."

Henry nodded and turned to climb the mast to help the sailor.

John watched him, proud of the kind and warmhearted man his son had become.

"Take us into the bay!" John hollered to Benjamin.

"Aye, sir! It's good to be back under your command, Cap'n."

"It's good to be back *in* command, Benjamin! Let's see what she can do on the open sea."

The six-week voyage took more out of John than he anticipated. He woke each morning stiff and sore. His face was sunburnt and his shoulders were covered with blisters. His stomach churned at the rotting rations of stored food. He wasn't used to the life of a sailor anymore. After the weeks of agony, John arrived in London tired and worn, wishing for his own bed and his wife. How did he do this so many times in the past? He had enjoyed watching his sons excel in sailing and admired their smiles, but he finally came to the conclusion that sailing at twenty-seven years of age was immensely different from sailing at fifty-seven years of age. Every bone in his body ached as he hobbled down the gangway, certain he looked like an old man. He breathed in the view—the bustling dock of Blackwall London that he hadn't seen for more than thirteen years. It hadn't changed much. Sailors, vagabonds, vagrants, whores—just as he remembered.

John spent the first two weeks setting up an office and warehouse in London. After accomplishing that goal, he traveled to Middlesex to visit with his sisters. He hadn't seen them in so long he was actually nervous and chastised himself for the quivering in his gut. They were his sisters, for goodness's sake. There was nothing to be nervous about.

He took a breath and climbed the stairs of Frances's palatial home. When Frances opened the door, she screamed his name and wrapped her arms around his neck, and all of his trepidations vanished. It was as if no time at all had passed. Cicely poked her head around the corner, and when she saw John, she joined the hug. Indeed, the women's outward appearances had changed, but their interaction with each other instantly reverted back to how they behaved when they were children all living under the same roof. Frances was her usual talkative self, asking a million questions about John's arrival and his family. Cicely grinned at him, but as they sat in the parlor, John noticed she looked frail.

"How are you feeling, Cicely?" he asked her.

"Not so well these days. I think old age is taking its toll on me."

"You're not the only one. I found it quite difficult to be on a ship for six weeks."

After a pleasant and much overdue visit with his sisters, John traveled down to Leeds Castle to check in on his nephew Alex. He found Alex happy and full of life, trotting about the castle like he was the baron who owned it. John hadn't been to the castle since he had rescued his family thirteen years earlier. At the time, it was overgrown with weeds and sorely neglected. Today, it was the most splendid place he had seen in a long time. Alex had transformed it into a grand home, and Lady Margaretta seemed very happy.

Following supper with Alex and Margaretta, John and Alex had a long and private conversation about Margaretta's abandonment by her husband. John hadn't paid any mind to the fact that Alex and Margaretta seemed very close, but now that he knew Thomas was nowhere to be found, John felt he needed to say something to Alex. Over their second glass of wine in the reception room, John broached the subject. "Please tell me you're not having an affair with her, Alex. Lord Thomas will have your head."

"Lord Thomas hasn't been here in three years. He lives in town with his mistress. It's no secret; Margaretta knows all about them. Lord Thomas is so wrapped up in that whore, he didn't even attend the reading of his father's will. I penned JC's will and was the witness of his last testament. Lord Thomas didn't even show up."

"I understand that he isn't the most respectable of the Culpepper men, but committing adultery with your cousin's wife doesn't say much for you, either. What would your mother say?"

"My mother is long dead, Uncle." Alex looked down at the floor for a moment and then back up at John. "And while I appreciate your concern, at thirty years of age, I think I'm old enough to do as I please."

John shook his head. "This could cause a family scandal."

"No, it won't. Lord Thomas couldn't care less about Margaretta's well-being. JC asked me to stay here and take care of her, and that's exactly what I intend to do."

"At your age, you should be married with your own children."

"I can't marry the woman I love if she is married to another."

John sighed. Nothing more could be said.

The last thing John did in London before heading back to Virginia was visit All Saints Church in Hollingbourne. He stopped at the front door and touched the Culpepper crest that was chiseled in stone to the left of the door. His family used to be important; he didn't think they were anymore. Lord Thomas had inherited the remaining Culpepper wealth from JC, but Lord Thomas was about the only example of aristocracy that remained. Not such a great example.

John opened the church's heavy wooden door, stopped for a moment to allow his eyes to adjust to the dim light, then weaved through the pews toward the chapel where the Culpeppers were buried. His father's tomb was the first he saw. He had never spent any time grieving over the loss of his father. At the time of his death, John was busy with a new merchant business and a young family and he thought his father's death wasn't such a great loss, but today a wave of melancholy, of lost childhood, of missed opportunities, of loneliness washed over him. He glanced around the church to make sure he was alone before he spoke.

"Hello, Father. I hope you are looking down on us and know all that has happened, for there is far too much for me to tell you." A tear rolled down his cheek as he pictured his formidable father gracing the head of the family dining table, ordering servants about, running their farm and household. He seemed to remember the smell of his father's shirt as he was held close, but he couldn't pinpoint exactly when that was. He didn't remember hugging the man when he was small. He had a vision of seeing his father smile at his mother. He loved her so and she loved him in return. What would life have been like if his mother hadn't died when he was a small child? John stood with his hand resting on the tomb for a long time, a million memories passing through his mind.

Finally, he turned to look for JC's tomb. He heard there had been an epitaph placed by JC's children, and when he found it and read it, he smiled. His dear cousin was very loved by both the elders of the family and his children. The epitaph read:

To the lasting memory of John, Lord Culpeper, Baron of Thoresway, Master of the Rolls and Privy Counsellor to two kings, Charles the First and Charles the Second. For equal fidelity to the king and kingdom he was most exemplary, and in an exile of above ten years was a constant attendant and upright Minister to the Prince last mentioned. With him he returned triumphant to England on the 29th of May 1660, but died the 11th of July in his 61st year of age to the irreparable loss to his family. He commended his soul to God, his faithful Creator, and ordered his body here to expect a blessed resurrection. His Patent of Honor from King Charles the First dated the 21st of October 1644 may serve as his immortal epitaph.

"Oh, JC, what a life you have lived," John ran his fingers over the chiseled words. "You always wanted to serve the king, and you outdid yourself in the position. I'm glad you're now at rest."

John left the church feeling worse than he had ever felt in his life. Memories of his father and his childhood created a sadness in him that encircled him like a shroud. The thoughts of the strength of his father, the intelligence of his brother, and the remarkable life JC had lived all made John feel lowly and inadequate. How did he ever end up as the patriarch of this family? He was never trained for such a job and certainly was not worthy of the honor. Yet, he was helping his sons create a merchant business. His nieces and nephews were doing well, as long as Alex didn't lose his head over matters of the heart. He had a nice visit with his sisters. And he was soon going back home to his wife. Maybe he *was* doing a good job. Maybe he shouldn't be so hard on himself. The rational thoughts still couldn't shake his sour mood.

John spent a few more weeks in England to make sure James was comfortable with the business and had found a nice place to live. When he was confident James would be fine, he hugged him good-bye and promised to see him again soon.

By the time John and the boys arrived back in Accomac, Denny and Robbie had made the decision to open a merchant route to Barbados. John offered to help them set it up, but had decided he would soon stop sailing. It was a young man's endeavor, and though John's head and heart loved every minute of it, his body told him otherwise.

Mary was thrilled with her husband's decision.

John Culpepper, Esquire

CHAPTER 22

1664, Storms

John and Henry made one final sailing to London in the spring of 1664. They visited Cicely, who looked even worse than the last time John saw her. They visited Alex, who was still living in sin with the beautiful Margaretta. They checked in on James, who was taking the family business to new heights.

They sailed back to Virginia on June 29 with an expected landing date of August 10.

The first four weeks of the voyage was without incident, but as they neared the coast of America, John saw blackening skies on the horizon and knew they were headed into rough weather.

He called to Benjamin in the crow's nest. "Benjamin, can we go around this? Do you see any clear skies ahead?"

Benjamin, holding a brass spyglass to his eye, replied, "No, Cap'n, I don't see a break in the storm in any direction."

"Is it heading toward us?"

"Aye, Cap'n, it is."

"Pull the sails. We'll wait it out."

Benjamin shouted commands at the crew and the sails quickly dropped. Sailors coiled ropes and tied the sails to the yardarms as the first rumble of thunder sounded.

Henry joined his father on the deck. "Is this a bad storm, Father?"

John looked forward to the ominous sky. "I've never seen anything like that. The sky is black."

A wave lifted the ship and Henry fell into his father.

John caught him by the arms. "Henry, go below and stay there. There's nothing you can do up here on deck."

Obediently, Henry turned and walked away, staggering like a drunken man with each pitch and roll of the ship.

John exhaled. This was not good. In all his years of sailing, he had never seen the sky this dark and he had never seen an expanse of clouds that block their way like this. This storm was immense in size. John hoped it didn't match in intensity. In the distance, a water spout rose from the surface of the ocean to the clouds above. Benjamin walked passed John, hollering commands to the crew to tie everything down, and he stopped yelling and froze in front of John to look at the water spout.

Without turning around to face John, Benjamin said, "Captain, we're in for a rough ride. We should all go below until this passes."

John nodded but he didn't move. He was mesmerized by the sight before him. The ocean had transformed from glittering blue to black. The crashing waves sent white foam spewing into the air. There was no horizon, just black water and black sky. Fat raindrops began to darken the deck, changing the light brown wood to a dark mud color. A forty-foot wave crashed into the bow, splashing buckets of water over the railing onto the deck. An inch of water flowed passed John's feet as the ship rocked backwards. Within a moment, the water came rushing back as the ship rocked forward. The storm quickly grew in intensity and suddenly fifty-foot waves began to smash into her sides, rocking her in uneven circles, as if riding on a wild, bucking horse. John held onto the thick pole of the main mast, watching anything that wasn't tied down disappear over the sides of the ship and into the blackness of the water. The thunder boomed and the rain began falling harder, coming down in sheets. John gave up his watch and went below with his men.

"Father, how long will this last?" Henry asked.

John shrugged, not willing to raise his voice loud enough to be heard over the raging storm.

Thunder that sounded like cannons

roared all around them. Lightning cracked every few moments, illuminating the interior of the hold through the cracks in the planks above the men's heads. Unsecured cargo and crates crashed against the sailors with every lurch of the ship. Water poured in through the cracks and the doorway as if they were directly underneath a waterfall.

John looked around at his men, wondering if they would survive this storm. The rise and fall of the waves was so strong, they could easily sink the ship. The ship bounced around like a stick floating down a stream. Everyone was soaked to the bone. Some faces were pale; one sailor threw up from the movement. John's men were used to storms, and had ridden out many over the years, but this one was a monster.

They rode the storm throughout the night with waves reaching upwards of eighty feet. Thunder reached a fevered pitch, pulsating through the ship with the roar of cannon fire. Lightning crackled above them, lighting the inside of the ship as if daylight had come. The winds rocked the ferociously, nearly capsized them. After surviving nearly ten hours of the frightening ordeal, the storm stopped as quickly as it had started. The winds hushed their roar, the sky lightened with the rising sun, the waves settled. Everything below deck was ruined. Their food stores were saturated with sea water. Their clothing and bedding were soaked. They soon realized they had been blown hundreds of miles off course, but the ship was in one piece and they were alive. They raised what was left of their tattered sails and finally arrived on the shores of Accomac on August 24.

Upon their arrival, they were told that storms had been plaguing the entire eastern seaboard of the colonies the whole summer. Roads were flooded, crops were washed away, homes were damaged. Mary was beside herself with worry that Denny and Robbie had sailed to Barbados and not been seen or heard from in months. The boys had been expected to return in June, but no one knew if the *Culpepper* had ever left Barbados, and if it had, where it was now. There was nothing they could do but wait. And pray.

Henry sent a stable boy to John's house to deliver a letter that Elizabeth had delivered John and Mary's first grandson in Portsmouth. The good news took Mary's mind off worrying about Denny and Robbie. She read the short message while sitting across from John at the dining table.

"John, who would have ever thought we'd have a grandchild born in Virginia?"

"When we married so many years ago, who would have ever thought we'd live in Virginia?"

"Well, I'm happy to be here with you. It has been quite an adventure being your wife."

He rose from his chair and knelt down

next to her. "My dear wife, I've loved every moment of it. Can I escort you to Portsmouth in the morning to meet your new grandson?"

She nodded and wrapped her arms around his neck.

The next morning, as John was hitching the mare to his old wagon, Berkeley appeared. He had been in a hurry, evident by the sweat on his horse, and his wrinkled brow told John something was terribly wrong.

Berkeley climbed down from his steed and didn't bother with greetings or pleasantries. "John, I'm afraid I have some bad news for you. A ship was found wrecked on the rocks off the coast of Carolina. From every indication, the sailors who found it think it's the *Culpepper*."

John's knees gave way and he found himself sitting on the ground, still holding the mare's reins.

Berkeley bent down and offered his hand. "I'm so sorry to be the bearer of bad news. The storm surge in that area was so bad last week, no one could have made it to shore. As far as anyone knows, there weren't any survivors." He took John's elbow and helped him stand.

Mary, not knowing Berkeley was there, bounced out of the house holding John's hat. "John, are you ready to go? You forgot your hat." She closed the door, saw Berkeley, and at the same time, saw her husband's pale face. "What happened?"

Berkeley looked at John, waiting for him

to speak, but he didn't. He looked back at Mary and frowned. "I'm afraid I'm the bearer of horrible news."

Mary stepped down the porch steps and cautiously walked toward the men. "What news? What happened?"

Berkeley looked at John again.

"Will, what happened?" Mary prodded, feeling a chill run up her spine.

"I'm afraid the *Culpepper* was found shipwrecked off the coast of Carolina."

Mary's eyes grew wide. "My sons?" she muttered.

Berkeley shook his head.

Mary looked at John and her eyes, filling with tears, transformed from shock to anger. "You did this."

John looked at her for the first time and shook his head.

"Yes," she continued. "You did this. You bought them that ship. You sent them to Barbados. You are responsible." She looked back at Berkeley. "Were their bodies recovered?"

"No, I'm afraid there wasn't much left of the ship. It broke apart on the rocks."

"How am I supposed to bury my boys?"

"There's nothing to bury, ma'am," Berkeley said.

John remained quiet, not even listening to the exchange between his friend and his wife. The last thing he heard was, "You are responsible." He knew she was right. He was responsible. In his struggle to be a good father, he somehow pushed his sons into his chosen profession. He wasn't as adamant as his father had been when he'd pushed John into law, but John was the one who had encouraged them. They wouldn't have been out there if he hadn't bought the ship. In trying so hard to *not* be like his own father, he had murdered his own sons.

Mary's silence and anger continued until the next day when she handed John a letter and told him to go down to the dock and find someone to deliver it to England. "I've written James about his brothers. We also need to go down to Henry's and find Johnny to tell them."

Johnny was somewhere in Carolina with his friends and seldom came home. John wasn't even sure where to look for him.

Without a word, John took the letter from his wife and rode down to the dock. The next morning, they traveled to Portsmouth to give Henry the bad news and to see their new grandson. As they rowed their small boat across the mouth of the bay, John looked out at the horizon and saw a beautiful merchant ship with her white sails billowed. He face turned pale and he closed his eyes.

"What is it, John?" Mary asked, her first civil tone in days.

"You were right. It is my fault." Tears filled his eyes. "It's my fault Denny and Robbie are lost. If I hadn't become a sailor, they wouldn't have followed in my footsteps."

"No, I owe you an apology, John. I was angry and hurt and I took it out on you. The storm was not your fault. The shipwreck was not your fault. You didn't make the decision to sail in that weather. And if you hadn't become a sailor, we'd all be dead in England right now at the hands of Cromwell's army. Don't blame yourself for something that's not your doing. "

John was silent the rest of the journey.

When they arrived at Henry and Elizabeth's house, they met their grandchild. He was a blue-eyed boy with dark curly hair, a typical Culpepper. He looked into John's face and smiled. John's heart was so raw, the infant's love caused a floodgate of tears to open. Mary and Elizabeth took the babe into the house and left John and Henry alone on the porch steps. John sat down on the step and cried. Henry sat down next to him. They didn't say anything for a long time.

Finally, Henry said, "I've heard about the ship, Father. Berkeley came by yesterday and told me. Do you think they're really dead?"

John looked down at his boots and struggled to speak. "I don't know. It seems so."

"I should have been with them to protect them."

"Then you'd be dead, too, Henry. The sea is a fickle mistress. She can take your life in an instant."

"Well, I feel like I need to do something."

"There's nothing you can do. What's done is done."

"I can do one thing."

John looked at his son, wonder what he could possibly do.

"I've decided to name my son after Robbie. He will be called Robert Culpepper."

John felt tears come to his eyes again. He remembered the day he'd said those exact words about his own son, Robbie. Robert Culpepper had been a good boy.

Mary emerged from the house carrying the baby. "John, did Henry tell you his name?"

John nodded and tried to smile. This infant would never be a replacement, but he would certainly be loved.

* * *

If things could go from bad to worse, they did. Just after the first blustery snowfall in January, a letter from James arrived.

Dear Mother and Father,

My heart is broken at the loss of Robbie and Denny. I can't imagine ever coming back to Virginia and them not being there. I'm so sorry.

I'm afraid I have more devastating news. Father, you had mentioned that Aunt Cicely didn't look well the last time you were in town. I'm afraid you were right. She died on November 5 and has been buried with all the dignity and respect she deserved at Westminster Abbey. Aunt Frances is beside herself. I'm going to go up to her house next week for a few days. I'll write more after the visit.

> *With all my love,*
> *James*

John had lost his only brother, two of his sons, and now his dear sister. He could barely get out of bed. As a child, he always imagined that growing up and becoming an adult would be the best thing that could ever happen. He could get out from under his father's strict rule. He could live his life the way he wanted with no one to dictate otherwise. But no one told him growing older came with its own painful problems. It certainly wasn't turning out as great as he thought it would be. Being the family patriarch was an impossible role to fulfill. He wondered how his grandfather did it. He wondered how his father did it. How could John be strong for everyone else when his insides were shattered?

CHAPTER 23

1667, Albemarle, Carolina

Three years had passed since that horrible, stormy summer that took the lives of Robbie and Denny. John and Mary had settled into acceptance and forgiveness. They found themselves on the other side of the tragedy, living a comfortable if not quiet life. They visited their grandson occasionally, and a few times a year they ventured to Jamestown to visit with Berkeley. Other than those infrequent trips, they worked on their farm, spent quiet evenings by the fireside, and eased into what most would consider old age. They had both just passed sixty years, and though they were in good health, they didn't care to venture out much. Losing their children took the spark out of their lives. James visited occasionally from England. Twenty-three-year-old Johnny had been seen only once or twice over the last few years. He made his home in Carolina, in the county of Albemarle.

They hadn't seen their nieces at all, and everything seemed to be quiet with Alex in England.

One afternoon, a messenger appeared at John's door and announced himself as a servant of Sir Samuel Stephens and Madam Frances Culpepper Stephens. He handed John a letter. As John looked down at the paper, the servant said, "Sir Stephens is to be appointed governor of Albemarle. He and his wife wish you to attend the festivities."

John thanked the messenger, opened and read the invitation, and then walked out to the garden to share the news with Mary. He found her pulling beans from the tall vines and handed her the letter. He watched as she read it.

She wiped the sweat from her brow with her wrist. "Our Frances, the first lady of Carolina?"

"Yes, ma'am. I married her off right well, didn't I?" He grinned.

"You certainly did, husband. Are you going to go?"

"Why don't we go together?"

"I can't leave. I need to take care of this garden. It's overgrowing with weeds."

"It's not that bad. It can survive a couple weeks without us."

She considered it for a moment. "Do you think we'll see Johnny while we're there?"

"Yes, I'm sure he'll be there. The whole town will be there. And we should make sure he's doing well. He's probably running the streets like a buck in rut. We should make sure he's not being goaded into causing trouble by those ruffians he associates with."

"He's probably goading them. You know he's fearless. Just like you."

John took the letter back and folded it. "Well, what do you think? Shall we pack?"

She picked up the bowl of green beans and looked at John. "We're going to starve when we return and find the weeds have taken over our garden, but I would love to go and see my son."

"Then let's go."

* * *

The following week, John and Mary paddled down the Chowan River, passing a few farmers who were navigating the waterway, taking their crops to market. There were a few small homes on the banks of the river, but mostly there were only trees. Very few settlers had ventured this far south, as the area was known to be inhabited by Indians.

"Why would anyone want to live this far south?" Mary asked.

"I heard they have better soil and far less frost than Jamestown, or perhaps they enjoy less taxes and more freedom down here."

"Then why do we always hear of Johnny joining in heated debates over those things?"

"I don't know, dear. I guess we'll find out when we get there."

After an arduous journey, they finally arrived at a point where there were two congested settlements, one on each side of the river, adjoined by an extensive bridge. John tied up their boat, found an inn, and the couple enjoyed a warm meal and a soft bed.

The next day, they walked across the bridge to attend the reception at the governor's house in the middle of town. The house was larger than any other in the village, but nothing compared to every home in Jamestown. John and Mary found the small rooms filled with well-wishers. They searched the rooms for the new governor.

"Sam!" John found him and shook his hand. "Congratulations on your new appointment."

"Thank you, John. I'm very pleased. Have you seen your niece yet?"

"No, I'm afraid not."

"Let me find her for you. She's around here somewhere, playing the gracious hostess, as always." Stephens made his way through the crowded room.

As John watched Sam saying hello to other visitors, his eye caught a young man entering the room. The man wore a wide-brimmed felt hat with a white feather sticking up from the band, his curly hair tangled in his collar. John nudged Mary. They watched him weave through the crowd, greeting other guests with a broad smile that resembled his father's.

John chuckled. "He's quite popular here. Looks like *he's* the newly appointed governor instead of Sam."

"He looks healthy and happy," Mary said with an air of relief.

"Johnny!" John called across the room.

The young man turned and saw his parents. He excused himself from the man he was talking with and hurried over. "Mother!" He kissed her on the cheek.

John patted him on the back. "You look great! How are you, son?"

Johnny gave his father a hug. "I'm good. I didn't know you would be traveling down here. I'm happy to see you both."

"You can always travel up to our house, you know," Mary quipped.

Johnny blushed. "I know, and I'm sorry I haven't come to see you more, but I've been very busy here in Albemarle."

After they had a few moments of small talk, Stephens returned with Frances.

"Frances, my dear, how good to see you," John said.

Mary hugged her. "Congratulations on your husband's appointment. Will you be staying in Albemarle?"

"Oh, heavens, no. I'll be returning to Jamestown just as soon as I can. I have no patience for the mosquitoes or the Indians."

John laughed. He'd never thought his niece had much patience for anything. She was now a grown woman but nothing else about her had changed.

* * *

Later that evening, John and Mary had a quiet supper with Frances and Stephens. Following the meal, John and Stephens dismissed themselves from the dining room for a drink in the parlor.

"John, I need to mention something to you," Stephens said after he cleared his throat.

"Sounds serious."

"It might be. I'm not sure. It seems your son is causing, or attempting to cause, quite a commotion in town over the taxes we've set into place. I haven't spoken with him directly about the allegations, but I keep hearing that he drinks in the pub almost nightly and loudly complains of our laws and tariffs. Other young men are beginning to follow his lead, and as a group, I think they could cause a lot of damage with their words. We're trying hard to grow this settlement. I'd hate to have anyone put a damper on it with their rebelliousness."

"Well, Sam, I won't deny what you're hearing. I haven't spoken with Johnny in a long time, but I know he has a streak of rebel in him. I wouldn't be surprised if what you're saying is true."

"I'm wondering if you would speak with him and ask him to tone down his arguments. I'd hate to begin my tenure with a settlement run amok, and I'd hate to have to silence him with force. He's family."

"I'm afraid I can't intervene at this time. Mary wants to head back to Accomac in the morning, and honestly, I don't even know where to find the boy. He's quite secretive when it comes to his whereabouts. Always has been."

"All right, then. I just thought I'd ask. If I have to do anything about him, Frances would murder me, and we both know she's the one who's really in charge around here." Stephens laughed.

John smiled. Yes, that fact was no secret.

The following morning, John and Mary left Albemarle without seeing Johnny.

CHAPTER 24

1668, Anna Culpepper Danby

"Aunt Mary, Lady Thornton told everyone she's been financially supporting me and Christopher for the last twenty years. We haven't even been married twenty years. I don't know why she'd exaggerate like that, and I don't know how we're expected to maintain our social status with her belittling us," Anna complained.

Mary rose to pour more cider into their cups. "*Has* your husband's aunt been supporting you?"

"Well...yes, but not for twenty years, so she doesn't need to be so spiteful."

"That may well be, but I don't understand why she has been supporting you. When did this all start?" Mary sat down in the chair across from Anna.

Mary and John hadn't seen Anna much since they married her off to Christopher Danby years ago, but Mary thought her nearly-forty-year-old niece was aging rather well. There wasn't one streak of gray in her hair or a wrinkle on her face. She was still the same pretty girl they had brought over from England eighteen years earlier.

"I didn't tell you at the time because I knew Uncle John would be upset."

"Tell us what?"

"When Christopher and I married, someone turned his father's ear and said I had inveigled him into marrying me. His father was convinced the arrangement was merely a ruse to get to the Danby fortunes."

"That's absurd. Your uncle made a good marriage agreement with Christopher. There was no deceit."

"I know that and Christopher knows that, but his father heard rumors in the colony and right after we were wed, he disowned Christopher."

"Why didn't you tell us at the time? I'm sure your uncle could have straightened it all out with Christopher's father."

"Christopher asked me not to say anything. He didn't want to upset Uncle John after Uncle John spoke so highly of him in front of my mother. Instead of involving Uncle John, Christopher wrote to his aunt in England and asked her for help. She said she wouldn't get involved in dealings between the Danby men, but she would be happy to help us financially. She's been sending us money ever since."

"And now she has stopped?"

Anna nodded. "Apparently she sent a letter to Christopher stating that we have never once thanked her or shown her any kind of favor, so she's not sending any more money. Christopher said her pride is hurt, but truthfully, we think she's simply a senile crone who can't remember who we are or why she's sending us money, so my husband wants to go to England and remind her."

"How long are you going to stay in England, my dear?"

"Forever! He said we can't afford to live here in Virginia without her funds."

"Pardon my saying, but why doesn't your husband work?"

"The son of Sir Thomas Danby should work? Surely you jest. He wouldn't know how to find work if it bit him like a snake."

"Oh, Anna, what are you going to do?"

Anna looked down at her hands, folded on her lap. "First, I'm going to find the courage to tell Uncle John that I'm leaving." She looked up at Mary. "Then when I arrive in London, I'm going to grovel to old Lady Thornton and beg her for money so my husband and children will be taken care of in proper fashion. Then I shall find the best seamstress in London and have some new dresses made."

At that moment, John and Christopher entered.

"Well, here he is. I suggest you tell him

right now," Mary said.

"Tell me what?" asked John.

Anna looked from her aunt to her husband to her uncle. "We're moving back to England."

CHAPTER 25

1669, Samuel Stephens

John was escorted up the staircase of the palatial Boldrup Manor by a young servant girl. "M'lady is in the governor's bedchambers. She hasn't left his side since he became ill," the girl said as they walked down the long, dark hallway toward the back of the mansion. When she opened the door, Frances looked up from the side of the bed, her eyes red-rimmed. The room was dim with the heavy curtains drawn. There were no doctors, no servants.

"Oh, Uncle John. Thank you for coming." Frances rose from her chair beside the bed and came over to greet him. Even in her grief, she still moved like a queen gliding through a crowd of onlookers.

He took her icy hands in his own. "How is he?"

She shook her head and looked down at the floor, inhaling as she did so. John looked toward the bed where the forty-year-old man lay, his breathing shallow, his face so pale his skin was almost translucent.

Samuel Stephens was the first governor of any colony to be born in America, a native of Jamestown. He and Frances had lived a quiet life on the Boldrup plantation until 1662, when King Charles II established the province of Carolina and asked Stephens to serve as Commander of the Southern Plantations. The land of the Southern Plantations spread through southern Virginia and into Carolina, and Stephens found himself away from home more often than not, leaving Frances to run the plantation alone.

Following Governor William Drummond's resignation in 1667, Stephens was appointed governor of Carolina. He moved all his personal belongings to Albemarle and spent nearly all his time there, while Frances remained at Boldrup. The two were not close as husband and wife, yet what seemed to be only an agreeable business arrangement had worked well for them. As Stephens rose in power through appointments from the king, Frances rose right along with him through her activities in the colonies. She ran one of the largest plantations in the land and was the consummate hostess, wining and dining the colonial aristocracy.

John hadn't spent much time with them, as he had no desire to be in that circle. It reminded him of the Culpeppers of old, always in the midst of some political strategy. He was certain his father would have reveled in the camaraderie of the colonies' upper elite, and would've especially been pleased with Frances's political and social activism. She would've been his favorite granddaughter, of that John had no doubt. Now, with her husband on his deathbed, her future was questionable.

"Oh, Uncle John, what am I going to do?" A tear rolled down her cheek.

John didn't know if she was asking about the legalities of being a widow or about her husband's property or her future social status, so he decided to cover all angles. "Frances, my dear, don't worry about anything except yourself and Sam. I'll take care of the rest, especially all the legal obligations. Sam has a will, correct?"

She nodded.

"Then I'm sure everything is in order."

She sighed, released his hands, and returned to her husband's bedside.

John followed her. "His breathing is quite shallow. What does the doctor say?"

"He said it doesn't look like Sam has more than a few days, and he'll return sometime this afternoon to look in on him."

"Has he awakened at all?"

She shook her head.

"Have you been sitting here all morning? Why don't you go downstairs and get yourself something to eat? I can sit with him."

Frances looked up at him and appreciation crossed her face. "I think I shall do that. Thank you, Uncle." She rose and walked out the door without looking back.

John looked down at Sam. "Oh, Sam, I don't know what we'll do with that girl when you're gone. She's quite a handful." He chuckled. "But you already knew that." He sat quietly beside the bed for the rest of the afternoon, occasionally rubbing Sam's arm or hand, watching his chest go up and down with the shallow, rattled breaths.

Frances and John held vigil at Sam's bedside the entire next day. Late the following night, Sam's breathing stopped. John expected melodramatic Frances to scream or cry, but she stood silent next to the bed. After a few moments, she straightened her skirt and left the room. John didn't know what to make of it. He didn't know whether he should follow her or not. He decided to let her go, and he sat next to Sam until the sun rose.

The funeral for Governor Samuel Stephens was filled with the kind of reverence a man of his station deserved. Frances, dressed in black, her eyes hidden behind a thin black veil, was the hostess of the biggest gathering Jamestown had seen in years. Following that event, she told John she wanted to travel down to Albemarle and visit with Sam's constituents in Carolina.

John couldn't accompany her since his son Henry had recently announced the birth of his second child. John needed to go back to Accomac, pick up Mary, and take her to Henry's house. He hated to leave his niece alone in her grief and didn't want her venturing to Carolina alone. He explained to her that he couldn't accompany her, and he asked his friend, Will Berkeley, to escort Frances to the colonial events in Carolina. He was certain the governor of Virginia would be an acceptable escort for the widow of the governor of Carolina. Berkeley was happy to oblige.

At the memorial service in Albemarle, Berkeley stood before the Carolina council and acknowledged Stephens as a man of courage and great integrity, virtuous and loved, and a lover of the colony.

Showing his support as John asked him to do, Berkeley stayed within arm's reach of Frances for the three-day visit. He admired her fortitude and was impressed with the way she handled her husband's constituents. They seemed to admire her in return. If it wasn't admiration, it was certainly respect. Berkeley knew Frances was esteemed in social circles, but in the political arena, she was more powerful than Berkeley thought a woman could ever be. She was indeed the grand dame of the colonies.

CHAPTER 26

1669, Henry Culpepper, Jr.

John traveled to Accomac and collected Mary to take her to visit their newest grandson. They sailed their little boat across the mouth of the bay, and as the sun began its westward descent, they docked at Portsmouth. Henry met them at the pier.

"Mother!" He wrapped her in his arms, then shook his father's hand. "How are you?"

"We're both fine, Henry, but you look a little pale. Are you feeling all right?" Mary asked him.

Henry smiled weakly. "I'm well, Mother. Just a little tired with the new baby and all. Elizabeth is excited to see you, and your new grandson is doing quite well. He's growing by leaps and bounds already."

"I can't wait to see him!" Mary said.

On the ride to Henry's house, they spoke of the late Governor Stephens and all the events memorializing him. Henry expressed his sympathies toward his cousin, Frances, and assured his parents that Frances was young and still had a long and happy life before her. When they arrived at Henry's modest home, Elizabeth met them on the covered porch. She was holding the sleeping baby and five-year-old Robert stood beside her, clutching her skirt. "Robert, say hello to your grandparents," Elizabeth coaxed, patting him on the shoulder.

Robert stepped away from the safety of his mother and grinned shyly at John and Mary.

John's heart swelled with love as he knelt on one knee and held out his arms. "There's my boy! Come see your old grandpa." John remembered his own grandfather saying those very words to him when he was about the same age. His eyes misted at the thought.

Robert carefully climbed down the steps and then ran to John and wrapped his arms around John's neck.

"You're growing so fast. How old are you now?" John asked.

The boy held up five fingers.

"Five? Such a big boy." John stood up and ruffled the top of Robert's head, again reminded of his own grandfather doing the same thing to him. Yes, this was what life was about—each generation showing love to the next. Too bad it skipped a generation with his own father. Too bad his sons didn't experience this paternal love. John shook off the thought. He refused to let memories of his father ruin his day with his son and grandsons.

Mary kissed Robert's cheeks, patted him on the head, and then climbed the stairs to meet her new grandson. Elizabeth handed her the baby without hesitation. "This is Henry Junior," she said.

"Oh, Elizabeth, he's beautiful!" She caressed his cheek with her index finger.

"He's already quite a handful. When he's hungry, the whole colony knows it. He's loud and demanding." Elizabeth giggled.

"That's how our youngest was, too. Johnny wanted what he wanted when he wanted it. And he's grown to be even more impatient and demanding. Quite a rebel, that one."

"This one is going to be the same." Elizabeth took Mary by the arm and led her toward the door. "Come inside and let's get out of the sun."

The family shared supper and chatted about Accomac, Frances's widowhood, Johnny spending so much time in Carolina, Robert, Henry Jr., and the latest tobacco prices. When the evening died down, John and Mary crawled into bed in the small room at the back of the house.

Mary whispered to her husband in the darkness. "What are you all going to do tomorrow?"

"Henry said he wanted to take me and Robert fishing."

"That sounds like a nice day. I'm looking forward to spending the day with Henry Jr. Isn't he the cutest little thing?"

"Yes, dear. Both those boys are something special."

John kissed Mary on the cheek and rolled over on the lumpy mattress.

Mary stared at the ceiling, pleased that her husband seemed so content.

CHAPTER 27

1670, Frances and Will Berkeley

In early summer of 1670, John and Mary sat on the grounds of Will Berkeley's palatial estate of Green Springs and watched thirty-five-year-old Frances enter the formal garden through a draping arbor of wisteria and stroll regally toward her bridegroom. Sir William Berkeley, the sixty-five-year-old governor of Virginia, awaited her arrival at the far end of the garden. John wrinkled his brow at the two gazing at each other. He would never have imagined his niece marrying his oldest and dearest friend. He wasn't surprised by the union as they were a political match made in heaven, although he thought Berkeley far too old and settled in his ways for John's vivacious niece. Berkeley was the most respected politician in the land and Frances was the queen of the colonies. No woman held more power or prestige than she, and John knew Frances would wear the pants in the family. He also knew that would be fine with Berkeley, who would sit back and let his wife take the lead.

Following the ceremony, Frances and Berkeley asked John to travel to Carolina to represent Sam Stephens's estate to make sure Frances's business was in order. John, happy to watch out for his niece's affairs, traveled to Albemarle to petition the court.

"Hear ye, hear ye, the superior court of Chowan County is now in session," announced the clerk.

John sat in the front row on a wooden bench and watched the clerk hand a document to the judge. The judge looked at it for a moment, signed it, and handed it back to the clerk, who read it aloud. "This court held the fifteenth day of July 1670 at the house of Samuel Davis, for the county of Albemarle, in the province of Carolina. Presided by the honorable Peter Carteret, governor and commander in chief.

"Whereas Mr. John Culpepper, Esquire, attorney for Sir William Berkeley, Knight, and Captain General of Virginia, petitions this court for letter of administration on the estate of Captain Samuel Stephens, deceased, he putting in security to render the court harmless, is ordered that Mr. Culpepper have the orders of administration granted to him."

The judge slapped his gavel on the desk, ending the proceedings. The clerk handed John the signed document and that was it. John was now in charge of Samuel Stephens's estate, and Frances was richer in her own right than any woman who had ever graced the shores of America. Stephens died with no children to leave his estate to, so Frances inherited all of his vast land holdings in Virginia and Carolina, including the thirteen-hundred-fifty-acre plantation of Boldrup and the entire island of Roanoke. Her new husband would now attain all of her properties. The newlyweds were the wealthiest landholders in the colonies.

John Culpepper, Esquire

CHAPTER 28

1670, Catherine Culpepper

John stormed through the front door of his house and tossed the letter on the table. "When did I completely lose control of this family?"

Mary wiped her hands on her apron. "What family? What are you talking about?"

"*This* family!" He threw his hat across the room onto the chair and ran his fingers through his hair. "My niece has been forced to go back to England, my other niece is married to a man twice her age, my sons have been killed on a ship that I bought for them, my youngest hasn't been seen in ages, and now my nephew is causing the worst scandal ever to befall the Culpepper family."

Mary walked toward her husband. "John, what are you talking about? Your nephew? You mean Alex?"

"Yes, Alex! I told him to keep his hands

off that woman."

Mary shook her head. "Now I'm really lost. What woman?"

He picked up the letter and handed it to Mary.

Dear Uncle,

I hope this letter finds you all in good health. I spoke with James last week and he is well and sends his regards to you and Aunt Mary. He said to tell you to send more tobacco on your next shipment to London. The warehouse empties of it as fast as it arrives.

The real reason for my letter is to let you know that Margaretta has delivered a beautiful daughter. She and the babe are doing well. The baby, of course, was born with blue eyes and curly dark hair like a typical Culpepper. She is so beautiful and such a joy, already trying to roll over by herself, and she always awakes each morning with a smile. Leeds Castle has become a brighter and happier place with her presence. I am humbled and grateful for her. She has been honorably named Catherine Culpepper, after my dear departed mother.

With warmest regards,
Alex

Mary's hand rose to her chest and she

looked up at John. "Isn't that sweet? Catherine Culpepper. Our Katherine would be so honored."

"Honored that her son is causing a family scandal?"

"I don't understand what you're saying. Alex has been watching over Leeds Castle for ten years. I'm sure it's nice to have a baby to brighten the place. What's the problem?"

"The castle isn't the only thing he's been watching over. Margaretta's husband has been living with his mistress in London for the last ten years."

He watched Mary's face transform from confusion to understanding. "The baby isn't Lord Thomas's?"

John shook his head. "I saw Alex and Margaretta together the last time I sailed to London. They were eyeing each other like newlyweds, and I warned him to keep his hands off that woman. She is married to his cousin, for Christ's sake."

"What do you think Lord Thomas will have to say about this?"

"I'm sure he doesn't care much about Margaretta, but he's a spoiled child who would never allow anyone else to play with his toys, even if he isn't using them. He's probably furious. I think I need to travel to London to save Alex's neck from a noose. Lord Thomas Culpepper is far too powerful for Alex to battle alone."

"When are you going?"
"I think I should go as soon as possible."
"I think you should, too."

* * *

Six weeks later, John arrived at Leeds Castle and conveniently found Lord Thomas and Alex sitting in the parlor. The tension in the room was as thick as day-old porridge.

Thomas rose and shook John's hand. "John, it's good to see you again. What brings you to London?"

"Good afternoon, Lord Thomas." John looked down at Alex, who hadn't risen from his chair. "I came to check on my nephew." Alex looked visibly shaken and pale. He stared straight ahead and didn't acknowledge his uncle. "Just in time, apparently."

Thomas glanced at Alex with a smirk, then returned to his seat on the sofa. He crossed his legs, took his glass of wine from the side table, and bounced his foot up and down.

John sat in the nearest chair. A servant offered him a glass of wine and he gratefully accepted. After taking a sip, he asked, "So, what's new here in Maidstone? What brings you out to the country, Lord Thomas?"

Thomas clenched his jaw. "I came to check on my *wife*." He glared at Alex.

Alex continued staring across the room. The silence grew to be extremely uncomfortable.

After a moment, Alex spoke quietly, almost as if he were in a trance. "Don't act like you do this all the time, Thomas. We haven't seen you in two years. The last time you were here was for precisely one hour to check on your horses."

"That isn't the point. The point is she's still *my* wife."

Alex turned and looked out the nearest window. "I doubt she feels the same."

Thomas laughed. "It doesn't matter how she feels. She is my property, just like this house, just like those horses."

John remained silent.

Thomas continued. "She belongs to me. I wouldn't let you take my horses or live in my house without my permission. She is no different."

Alex looked him in the eye. He trembled with emotion and raised his voice. "I'm afraid she *is* different. She's not a piece of property. She's a woman, a lady with feelings. You unceremoniously dumped her here and walked away an entire decade ago, leaving her to live alone in this mausoleum. You haven't cared for her one bit for ten years, but now that someone else cares for her, you come barging in here with threats and demands."

The lawyer in John came to life. "Has Thomas threatened you, Alex?"

"Not in so many words, but his demeanor is nothing but threatening."

"On the contrary, my dear cousin," Thomas said in a condescending tone. "I've come to share some great news. I have been appointed a member of the Council for Foreign Plantations, and I'm here to offer you the position of Surveyor General of Virginia."

Alex's jaw dropped.

Thomas continued. "The thing is, you'll have to leave for Virginia at once. Since your uncle has conveniently appeared, it'll all work out for the best, as you can return to Virginia with him." He smiled slyly at John.

John shifted his eyes at Thomas. "What's the catch?"

"There's no catch. Alex accepts the position and goes to Virginia, and I'll forget he bedded my wife." His face turned deadly serious as he turned to look at Alex. "My name won't be dragged through the mud. We won't see your head on a spike. The baby won't be declared a bastard, and *my* wife won't be declared a whore. It works out for everyone involved."

Alex looked at his uncle.

John nodded that the offer was a good one.

"What about Catherine?" Alex asked, his voice cracked.

"What about her? I'll raise her as if she were my own. No one needs to know the difference." He waved his hand around the room in demonstration. "Margaretta and the bastard will continue to live in great splendor."

Alex exhaled and looked at the floor.

John and Thomas stared at him, awaiting a response.

Alex rose suddenly and offered his hand to Thomas. He did not meet his eye. "I'll go."

Thomas stood and shook Alex's hand. "Good. You have a safe journey." He reached for his hat. "Maybe I'll take the child to live with me in London. Any day now my mistress will deliver our child, and the two...um, siblings will certainly become the best of friends."

Alex looked as if he were sick to his stomach.

"It looks like our business is settled, then. Good day, gentlemen." Thomas nodded and left the room, not even bothering to ask about Margaretta or baby Catherine.

"Good day, Lord Thomas," John said as Thomas disappeared around the corner. John heard his cousin's heels click on the marble floor of the foyer and the front door close.

He shook his head at Alex. "He let you off easy. He could have had your head on a plate for what you've done."

Alex stood in the middle of the room, his shoulders slumped, staring down at the ornate rug.

"Pack your things and say good-bye to Margaretta and your daughter. We'll sail in two days. You need to come with me to Virginia and let this mess die down."

CHAPTER 29

1672, Fishing

John and Mary ventured down to Henry's. Their grandsons were now three and eight, and there was nothing John enjoyed more than fishing with them. This would be the third time they called this summer. While Mary and Elizabeth visited at the house, John and Henry took the boys down to the bay for the afternoon. The four sat on the grass on the banks of the Chesapeake.

"Look at the ship!" exclaimed Robert, pointing at a large merchant ship across the bay. "Have you ever sailed on a ship, Grandpa?"

John chuckled. "As a matter of fact, I have. I've sailed across the ocean many times." John admired the ship before him and longed for his younger days when he had sailed into the sunset without a care in the world. Since Alex was now in Virginia and Anna was enveloped in the Danby family, unless there was an emergency, he knew he'd never sail again, and at the age of sixty-four, he figured that was probably a good thing. He loved sailing, but it was a young man's venture.

"Ship!" said Henry Jr., also pointing at the ship.

John looked down at the toddler next to him and smiled. He wouldn't trade this moment for a lifetime of sailing the seas. "Yes, ship. Isn't she beautiful?"

Henry Jr. nodded. He laid his head on John's leg and stuck his thumb in his mouth. The little one never lasted long while sitting on the bank, listening to the wavelets lapping the shore and the seagulls whistling overhead. John stroked the child's curly hair and soon the boy closed his eyes.

"Henry," John said. "You've got a couple special boys here."

Henry smiled. "I know. I love them to death. I have to tell you, though, I have a whole new respect for you. I don't know how you raised five of us. These two wear me out."

"Your mother did the raising. I was always at sea, if you'll remember."

"Yes, I remember, but I also know that when you were home, we never left your side. You always had us down at the ship or at the storehouse. We followed you around like little mice."

"Those were the best times. I always longed for you all to grow up and come on the ship with me."

"I know you did, but truthfully, I never wanted to sail. Sorry I couldn't give you that dream."

"That's all right. It was my dream, not yours." John looked over at Robert, who was reeling in his line and then casting it back into the water. "I never wanted you to follow my dream. Look what happened to Robbie and Denny."

"No, Father, they didn't follow your dream. They wanted to sail."

John looked down at the water. "I still feel responsible. If I didn't sail, they never would have, and they wouldn't have died."

"If you didn't sail, what would you have done when you were young?"

"I guess I would have been a lawyer like I've been doing for the last twenty years. That's what my father wanted me to do."

"You're a good lawyer. You've always been fair and logical."

"I always hated the thought of other lawyers and their rhetoric, of shuffling papers and arguing policies. Throughout my entire youth and even while in the middle of law school, I dreaded the thought of becoming a lawyer. I always wanted to sail a ship."

Henry looked at Robert staring at the ship in the distance. "It looks like your grandson may have the same desire."

"Well, if I can give you any words of

wisdom, which I know were far and few between in your youth, let your sons grow up and do what they want."

"I appreciate your allowing us to do that, but what happens when one of them decides to follow a not-so-good path? I'm thinking of Johnny in particular."

John shook his head. "Johnny's just headstrong. If he uses his rebellious trait for good, he can do something great. Men like him change the world. Their lives are never neutral. If he uses his nature for evil, well, then he'll have to pay the price somewhere along the way. There's nothing I can do to change the path he has chosen. Even as a parent, if you try to push your agenda onto your children, you'll end up with children who hate you like I hated my father."

"Do you still?"

"Hate him? I don't know. If it weren't for him demanding that I go to law school, I wouldn't have been able to care for my family the last twenty years. Maybe things always work out for the best, and maybe the fact that you don't see eye to eye with someone is no reason to hate them."

Henry looked across the water. "Did you learn that in law school?"

"I learned that through experience, I guess."

"You've been a great father."

A tear came to John's eye. "And you're a

great son."

THE END

Lori Crane

Author's Notes

This book stems from decades of genealogical research by me and others. I found that in the late 1500s, there were more than a dozen Culpepper barons and earls living in England. They had enormous wealth, vast land holdings, and great manor houses, many of which are still standing today. This was the privilege John Culpepper was born into and is detailed in the first book of the Culpepper Saga, *I, John Culpepper*. I wondered how and why, when they possessed such great power and prestige, they chose to sail across the ocean, move to an inhospitable land, and face possible starvation and death. Why would they leave the comfort of their manors and servants to live in probable squalor and battle savage Indians? How did they end up becoming the modest people I knew in my youth in Mississippi? We discovered the answers to those questions in the second book of the Culpepper saga, *John Culpepper the Merchant*, when a disastrous civil war in England ran the royalist family off its land. The Culpeppers had no choice but to leave, and probably with only the clothes upon their backs.

As I researched the family, I ran into the problem most Culpepper researchers encounter. Each man named John had a brother named Thomas. Each John and Thomas had sons named John and Thomas. As the family grew, cousins and second cousins were all named John and Thomas, and they occasionally married within the family, creating a whole new tangled web of Culpepper history. The records blurred. The history became confusing. English records were destroyed. Colonial records were incomplete. After committing the known timelines of all of the different Johns and Thomases to paper, I believe I have sorted out which one was which. In an attempt to keep them straight in the reader's mind, I have given some of them nicknames, yet they are all listed in historical records as John or Thomas. Of course, as new documents are uncovered, it is possible that my theory is just as mistaken as theories that have come before.

John Culpepper the merchant was the first in the family to migrate to America. This four-book series begins on the day John was born and concludes at the end of his life, but John's is not the only story here. There are far too many religious and political events and bold and brave personalities surrounding the family to ignore. These events and people shaped the man we know as John Culpepper. This series uncovers a life of passion, heroism and bravery, love and forgiveness, and ultimately truth. Truth of our history and truth about life itself.

John Culpepper is believed to be the progenitor of all American Culpeppers. He was my tenth great-grandfather. His son Henry was my ninth. His grandson Robert was my eighth.

There are many historical records in Virginia and Carolina of John's eldest son, Henry, and his youngest son, John, whom I call Johnny in this series and who is prominently featured in the fourth book of the Culpepper saga, *Culpepper's Rebellion*. Unfortunately, there are no records of John's middle sons, Denny or Robert, after August 1664 in Virginia. At that time, they would have been twenty-seven and twenty-three, respectively. Records show John's other son, James, in London and returning to Virginia in 1665, 1667, and 1670. After that, there are no further records of him ever returning to Virginia. Contrary to my tale, there are also no known records of John's wife ever entering Virginia. It is possible she died en route from England in 1650 or maybe even during the English civil war.

Not included much in this story is John's nephew, Thomas's son, who was also named John Culpepper and referred to as JJ at the beginning of this book. This young man stayed in Virginia after his father's death and rose to become Surveyor of Virginia and eventually the High Sheriff of Northampton County, Virginia, in 1673. He died in 1674 leaving no heirs in his will. He is often confused with our hero John Culpepper, but our hero had known heirs and would have been an aged sixty-seven when the sheriff records began.

There is also a bit of confusion over a 1664 record of a man name John Culpepper entering Virginia with three small sons. The boys—Thomas, Dennis, and Robert—were listed as being born in 1659, 1660, and 1661. It's unlikely this is our hero, as his sons Dennis and Robert were born in 1637 and 1641, and John would have been fifty-eight at the time of the document, a bit aged to start a new family with sons of the same names. If it is our hero in the records, he must have married a younger woman, or the birthdates on the document were written incorrectly. The document probably wasn't about John's youngest son, either, as Johnny would have only been fifteen when the first child was born. If it was John's nephew JJ, son of Thomas, why were these children not mentioned in his 1674 will? Unless, of course, their deaths predated JJ's own. It may have been John's son James, named incorrectly on the docket or transcribed incorrectly by researchers, as James would have been twenty when the first child was born and could have brought the children over to America to visit his father. I'll leave this dilemma for other researchers to figure out.

My deepest thanks go out to those who made this book possible:

Elyse Dinh-McCrillis — TheEditNinja.com
Robert Hess — book designer

Warren Culpepper and Lew Griffin, who maintain the Culpepper Connections website, and all of the Culpepper descendants who contribute to it.

Lori Crane

Books by Lori Crane

Okatibbee Creek Series
Okatibbee Creek
An Orphan's Heart
Elly Hays

Stuckey's Bridge Trilogy
The Legend of Stuckey's Bridge
Stuckey's Legacy: The Legend Continues
Stuckey's Gold: The Curse of Lake Juzan

Culpepper Saga
I, John Culpepper
John Culpepper the Merchant
John Culpepper, Esquire
Culpepper's Rebellion

Other Titles
Savannah's Bluebird
Witch Dance
The Culpepper-Fairfax Scandal
On This Day: A Perpetual Calendar for Family Genealogy

Lori Crane

About the Author

Bestselling and award-winning author Lori Crane is a writer of southern historical fiction and the occasional thriller. Her books have climbed to the Kindle Top 100 lists many times, with *Elly Hays* debuting on Amazon at #1 in Native American stories. She has also enjoyed a place among her peers in the Top 100 historical fiction authors on Amazon, climbing to #23. She is a native Mississippi belle currently residing in greater Nashville.

She is a member of the Daughters of the American Revolution, the United States Daughters of 1812, the United Daughters of the Confederacy, and the Historical Novel Society. She is also a professional musician and member of the Screen Actors Guild-American Federation of Television and Radio Artists.

Visit Lori's website at
www.LoriCrane.com

Sign up for Lori's quarterly newsletter at
http://eepurl.com/GHJ7D

Excerpt from

Culpepper's Rebellion

the fourth book

in the Culpepper Saga

Lori Crane

CHAPTER 1

1680, The Tower, London

John followed the guard down the winding hallway. It was narrow and dark with only the light of an occasional torch resting in its iron holder, flickering shadows on the stone walls. Where John could see, the walls looked dark and damp, covered with a slimy layer of green mold, but the musty smell didn't mask the overwhelming stench of urine and feces. He shook his head and wrinkled his nose at the insult.

As he passed intermittent arched doorways, prisoners yelled at him through small, bar-covered windows and pounded their fists on the wooden doors. Some begged for mercy, others pleaded for food and drink. The desperate voices echoing off the walls should have made John uneasy, but he only felt sheer hopelessness for those imprisoned. He didn't look up when they called to him. He walked behind the guard with his head down, his heart heavy. How could any man endure this dreadful place? He remembered his older brother serving a short sentence within these walls during the civil war more than thirty years earlier, but in all of John's seventy-four years, he had never seen the inside of the Tower. The unfortunate occasion that had brought him all the way from Virginia to be here on this day was more terrifying than the actual place.

The guard slowed when he rounded the corner, reaching inside his tunic pocket and noisily producing a ring of iron keys. John waited while the man found the appropriate key and placed it in the keyhole. When he turned it, there was a loud metallic snap. The guard pushed open the door, which moaned softly on its rusted hinges, and John entered.

The small room was lit by only a sliver of a window placed so high on the wall that none could see in or out. As the guard closed and locked the door behind him, John's heart melted at the sight of the figure lying in a ball on a wooden platform, facing the moldy wall. John assumed the platform was a bed, but there was no blanket, no warmth, no comfort. A mouse scampered across John's boot and disappeared into the tiniest of holes in the wall. At least the prisoners didn't have to sleep on the floor with the mice.

"Johnny?" John said quietly.

Johnny sat up and spun around. "Father! What are you doing here?"

"I came to see to your welfare."

"They've charged me with treason." He

ran his fingers through his disheveled curls.

"I know. That's why I'm here." His son looked so thin and worn. "You need a lawyer and I know of none better than myself."

"You hate practicing law."

"I'd hate it more to see your head on the scaffold."

"I don't think you can prevent it. They believe I embezzled the king's funds."

"Did you?"

"Of course not."

"Then we'll find a way out of this. Your mother will be very displeased with me if I allow you to lose your head."

Johnny rose and wrapped his arms around John. "Thank you for coming, Father. I hate to admit it..." He paused and swallowed hard. "But for the first time in my life, I'm truly frightened."

"I am too, son."

Made in the USA
San Bernardino, CA
22 July 2020